A sudden yea
the touch of h

"I'm Matt Donahue," he said. "Your closest neighbor. I was interested in buying this piece of land."

"I'm not selling." Corrie had already decided the place was hers. A place where her heart could be at home.

"You haven't heard my offer," he said mildly.

"Nor do I plan to." She saw no reason to tell him the land wasn't even really hers to sell, even if she wanted to. And maybe it never would be. How had she managed to overlook the fact that while her heart was saying *forever* to this little shack in the trees, a legal document said something else?

Husband required.

For a moment, having the *h* word in her mind at the same time that this big, handsome man with the strong, steady eyes filled her doorway made her almost helpless with longing…

Cara Colter shares ten acres in the wild Kootenay region of British Columbia with the man of her dreams, three children, two horses, a cat with no tail and a golden retriever who answers best to 'bad dog'. She loves reading, writing and the woods in winter (no bears). She says life's delights include an automatic garage door opener and the skylight over the bed that allows her to see the stars at night.

She also says, 'I have not lived a neat and tidy life, and used to envy those who did. Now I see my struggles as having given me a deep appreciation of life, and of love, that I hope I succeed in passing on through the stories that I tell.'

WED BY A WILL

BY
CARA COLTER

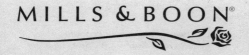

MILLS & BOON®

*First published in Great Britain 2003
Harlequin Mills & Boon Limited,
Eton House, 18-24 Paradise Road, Richmond, Surrey TW9 1SR*

© Cara Colter 2001

ISBN 0 263 83220 1

*Set in Times Roman 10½ on 12 pt.
01-0303-46731*

*Printed and bound in Spain
by Litografía Rosés, S.A., Barcelona*

Prologue

February 15...

With a sensation of panic, Corrine Parsons realized how close she was to crying. Glancing at the two women she had never seen before, yet whose identical faces were the same as the one she saw every time she looked in the mirror, she fought the emotions that threatened to capsize her control.

Triplets. She was one of triplets.

It didn't matter what the *precise* emotion she felt was, and she couldn't identify it. Was it gladness or sadness? Shock or just plain fear?

No matter what the emotion, she knew the first rule. She knew it by heart. The first rule was never to cry. Never.

She'd learned that for the first time when she was six, and had gone into her first foster home because her aunt Ella was ill. Terrified and so alone, she had been so happy when she had found the puppy.

She had secretly hidden him under the porch, stealing scraps from the garbage to feed him. And she had loved him, nursed him, played with him.

Then she had been discovered. The rules: No puppies—never, ever no matter how much you cried and pleaded. The tears flowing freely then, as she tried to make her foster parents understand how much it meant to her.

The truth: no one cared.

A truth underscored over the years: as her hand cramped from writing out "Thou shalt not steal" when she had not stolen anything.

When a foster mother's real daughter wore Corrine's red jacket, without even asking. That jacket had been the only nice thing she owned. *You should be glad to let her wear it, after all we've done for you.*

From age six to seventeen, she'd been in foster care on and off many times. Seven different foster homes had taken Corrine Parsons's tears and turned them to ice, cold hard ice that she saw in her eyes every time she looked at her own reflection in a mirror, even today, ten years after she had left her last foster home behind her.

Now, here she sat in a posh law office, with rich furnishings and thick carpets, surrounded by strangers, and the ice felt like the hot blue flame of a blowtorch was being aimed at it. Tears, hot and shaming, pressed behind her eyes. She had the terrifying feeling she might not be able to control whether they fell or not for very much longer.

And all because two of the strangers in this room looked exactly like her.

Were not strangers at all, though she had not met them before, at least not in her memory.

Sisters.

Mirror-image sisters. Triplets.

Back when she had still dreamed, as a lonely child—

with her few clothes in a plastic garbage bag at the end of yet another unfamiliar bed, had she not dreamed of such things? Had she not lain awake in the darkness and tried to soothe her own fears with dreams?

There had been detailed dreams of an imaginary family: A Christmas tree with gifts piled high beneath, gifts with her name on them. A bed with no crinkly rubber protecting the mattress. Sheets that felt soft instead of scratchy, and smelled of a mother's love. A strong, handsome father who threw back his head and laughed and picked up his little girl and swung her in the air. Sisters who shared Barbie dolls and hair ribbons and giggles and secrets.

Dreams...of someone to love her.

Corrie, she told herself firmly, as the tears pushed harder at the back of her eyes, these two women look like you, and they're your sisters. But that doesn't mean anything. It doesn't mean they will love you, or care about you, as if blood could automatically guarantee those things.

Still, when she dared to glance at them, at Abby and Brittany, she could see something in their eyes when they looked back at her. It was as if they hadn't even noticed she was not dressed appropriately. That she had purposely worn her oldest clothes in defiant answer to the summons that had arrived from the law office on creamy linen paper.

Her sisters' eyes held tenderness.

Welcome.

She wanted so badly to believe. And was terrified to believe at the same time. Her faded jeans had a hole in the knee, and she worked the frayed threads with her fingers, trying desperately to keep control of her world.

Far away she could hear the lawyer's voice going on and on. About a stranger giving them gifts. Huge gifts. Abby got a house. Brittany a business. Another man came in and went out again, but she hardly noticed.

She heard her own name. And her gift. Five acres of land. And a cabin. Her sisters looked naively happy, but she could feel herself bracing, waiting for the catch.

There was always a catch.

Sure enough, there it was. There were conditions attached to the gifts. If they wanted to keep them they had to stay here, in this little ocean-bound town she had never seen before, for one year.

And they had to get married within that year.

Married. Yeah, right. She, who had mastered the art of freezing a man where he stood with just one glance from her ice-cold eyes.

But if she came and lived here, even for that year, she could be with them. Her sisters.

See? It was happening already. She was nearly weak with wanting what she saw in their eyes.

What if she came, rearranged her whole life to be with them, and they didn't like her?

The fear was so intense it was like falling off a cliff, falling and falling and falling.

But suddenly, she wasn't falling anymore.

Her sister Abby slid her hand across the small space between their chairs, and intertwined their fingers. It was as if she *knew* the terror Corrie was feeling, and knew, too, how to make it go away.

Abby's hand was warm and soft and strong. She squeezed, and when Corrie looked up at her, what she saw in her sister's eyes made her realize she would be moving to Miracle Harbor, no matter how scared she was now. Not right away, of course. Corrie had obligations that had to be looked after first. But as soon as it was possible, she would come.

Frightened and excited at the very same time, Corrine

admitted the hardest thing of all. That she was powerless to stay away from these gifts that had been offered to her…the hope and the tenderness she saw shining in her sisters' eyes.

Chapter One

Three months later...

Hers.

Corrine shoved her hands in the back pockets of her jeans, and rocked back on her heels, studying the cabin. It stood, small and solid, under the spreading wings of a giant red maple.

Hers.

It didn't matter to her that the porch sagged, that the shingles on the roof had grown a thick layer of moss, that the windows were grimy and needed to be cleaned. It didn't matter to her that the second step was broken, or that the caulking was crumbling and rocks had fallen away from the top of the stone chimney.

She sighed, and allowed herself to feel a little finger of happiness. Nothing had ever really been hers before.

Of course she had owned clothing, and her beloved, if ancient Jeep that still had patches of its original green color in a few places.

But she had always rented an apartment in Minneapolis, even long after her moderate success with the *Brandy* picture book, Brandy being a young orphan girl of her creation who took on the world with spunk and fire and who always won.

Why hadn't she bought a house?

Maybe because it would be tempting fate to believe in good things, to commit to anything at all beyond a deadline.

Even feeling so good about this ramshackle cabin concerned her.

Nothing in her history allowed her to believe good things lasted.

"Well," she said out loud, and smiled, "according to sister Brit, this place doesn't qualify as a good thing. Not even close."

Brit had been appalled by the tiny cabin, the tumbledown barn, the falling-down fences that surrounded pastures gone wild, grass and weeds and wildflowers much higher than the fences.

"You can come live with me and Mitch," Brit had announced shortly after Corrie had finally arrived.

"You're newlyweds!" Corrie had said. Her sister had been married for only a week. She and her husband, Mitch, had hardly been able to keep their hands off each other long enough to say their vows. Corrie didn't want to live with that—evidence, cold hard evidence, that dreams came true, that miracles happened all the time.

Both her sisters were evidence of that, judging by the happiness they had found since coming to Miracle Harbor. The thought made terror claw in Corrie's throat.

Never cry, had just been the first rule. But the second rule was just as strong: *Don't hold hope.* Having hope could be the most dangerous thing of all.

"We'll come help you clean it up," Abby had declared bravely, staring at the cobwebs inside the little cabin, her face a ghastly shade of pale.

Corrie had been amazed that her sisters shared her terror of spiders, felt that funny warm spot around her frozen heart threaten to expand.

So, of course, she had refused their offers of help. But not just because she could not stand to owe anyone anything, and not just because she felt vulnerable in the face of her sisters' enthusiasm for her when they did not know the first thing about her.

Somehow cleaning the caulking was like claiming it. Making it hers in a way no one could take away from her. She took a deep breath, and glanced around.

There was work everywhere. The barn was practically falling down. The yard was nonexistent. Maybe she should start out here—

"Corrie," she told herself, "get in there. Or else you'll be sleeping outside tonight." She debated whether there would be more spiders inside or out.

She took a deep breath, skipped over the broken step, and gave the door a shove. It squeaked open.

The interior of the cabin was simplicity itself. One large room served as both the kitchen and the living room. The kitchen had a single row of cupboards, badly in need of paint, and a countertop badly in need of new Arborite. The rust-stained sink was the old porcelain variety. The fridge and stove, thankfully, looked new and spotless.

A doorway off the kitchen, with no door, led to a bedroom that looked like it had been added to the cabin as an afterthought. The tiny bathroom, too, must have been added later, since the cabin looked to be eighty or ninety years old, and the bathroom was modern, bright and clean.

A black potbellied stove in the center of the large room

cted as a divider between the kitchen and living room. On the other side was her living room, empty as yet. She liked its rough-hewn gray log walls, and the window, french-paned and huge. Once the window was cleaned she knew the light would be spectacular in this room. She would unpack her easel first, and put it right here where she could glance out the window at the wild grass and flowers, and the grove of trees and the leaning barn and know that everything she was looking at was hers.

A single beam of sunshine had found its way through the grime in the uncurtained front window, and it danced across the floor.

She went and stood in that sunbeam, scraped a layer of dust from the floor with the toe of her sneaker, and saw that the wood beneath was golden and warm.

Lost in thought, picturing bright yellow-checkered curtains at the windows, throw rugs on the floor, red tulips in a glass jar on the kitchen table, she did not hear him come in.

"Anybody here?"

She whirled around, gasping, some ingrained instinct spurring her to look for a weapon. Something to protect herself. Her mind raced back along the length of the long rutted driveway that led to her door. She was a long way from the nearest neighbor. No one would hear a cry for help.

There was nothing she could use to defend herself, and not even a coffee table to dart behind. A quick exit would do, she thought but then her mind started to kick in and she remembered. The movers. He had to be one of the movers. After all, she had been waiting for the movers to come with her meager scraps of furniture.

The light poured in the door behind him, and for a moment all she saw was his silhouette. She knew immediately he was not a furniture mover, yet her fear stayed at bay, and as she studied him she felt herself relax minutely.

Beige cowboy hat, white T-shirt, narrow-legged jeans on long, long legs, booted feet, broad, broad shoulders. Even without the hat, something would have whispered cowboy.

The confident angle of the chin, the solid plant of his feet, something in the way the muscle danced under the sunlight that glanced off the hair on his arms.

She didn't know there were cowboys in Oregon. Of course, she didn't really know very much about Oregon at all, except that the climate promised to be kinder than it was in Minnesota.

"I'm sorry, I didn't mean to startle you."

"You didn't startle me," she said, cool and defensive. But his voice had already penetrated those defenses. A deep voice, a sure voice. It only penetrated just enough for her to decide she was safe in this cabin, with a stranger who had appeared on soft feet, out of nowhere.

Her eyes adjusted to the light, and the details of him came clear to her. Brown eyes, steady, unwavering, calm and strong. A lot could be told from a man's eyes. It was a survival skill she had perfected, another remnant from her childhood.

His cheekbones were pronounced, and his nose looked like it might have been straight once. Now the perfection of his looks was marred by the bump where the nose had been broken, but oddly the flaw made his appearance infinitely more appealing than pure perfection might. The crooked nose proclaimed him a man's man, who lived in a man's world, and paid the price for it. He probably accepted his lumps with no more than a casual shrug.

He had a beautiful mouth. Her artist's eyes insisted on

seeing that; the sensuous fullness of the lower lip, the firm curve of the upper one.

He took a step toward her, his hand extended, and she backed up.

He lowered his hand slowly, and regarded her, the eyes narrow now, assessing.

Rule Three: *Never let them see your fear.* It didn't matter if she didn't even know why she was scared, why her heart was pumping rabbit-swift, and why everything in her knew the scariest thing she could have done would have been to accept that extended hand.

She knew exactly what it would feel like.

It would be warm, dry, infinitely strong and leather-tough. The touch of his hand would invite her to look into a world where people were not alone. Just a tantalizing glimpse, before he released his grip.

A sudden yearning leapt in her that she had to fight. A yearning that made an entirely different kind of fear breathe to life within her.

"What can I do for you?" she asked, her voice ice-cold, not a trace of any sort of emotion in it.

She knew he heard the coldness, though his reaction was barely discernible. A flicker in a muscle along the line of his jaw, a slight narrowing of his eyes that had the unfortunate effect of bringing the thick sooty abundance of his lashes to her attention.

"I'm Matt Donahue," he said, just the faintest hint of ice adding a raw edge to the warm timber of his voice. "I'm your closest neighbor," he nodded, "on that side."

If he expected the welcome-neighbor routine, she hoped to disappoint him. She said nothing, waited, after a moment, folded her arms across her chest.

"I actually was interested in buying this piece of land.

I heard someone had bought it before I even realized it had come up on the market.''

So he wasn't exactly here as part of the welcome neighbor routine, either. Surprise. Surprise.

''I'm not selling.'' See? That was what attachment did. She'd only just got here, and already she had decided the place was hers. A place where her heart could be at home. She felt inordinately angry at him for making her see how fragile places for the heart really were.

''You haven't even heard my offer,'' he said mildly.

''Nor do I plan to.'' She saw no reason to tell him she was in no position to sell, even had she wanted to. The land wasn't even really hers to sell, yet. And maybe it never would be. How had her heart managed to overlook that little detail when she was planning throw rugs and curtains and bright red tulips?

That while her heart was saying *forever* to this little shack in the trees, the legal document said something else.

Husband required.

For a moment, having the H-word in her mind at the same time that this big, handsome man with the strong steady eyes filled her doorwell made her almost helpless with longing.

Wishing that she could be a different person than she was. Softer and kinder, like her sister Abby or more outgoing and sexy like her sister Brit.

She felt her lack of warmth should have at least backed him out the door by now, but he stood, feet planted, regarding her thoughtfully, almost lazily. His eyes drifted casually to her bare ring finger, which gave her permission to take a swift, discreet glance at his.

His fingers were long and lean and ringless. Any kind of jewelry on them—even a wedding band—would have looked foolishly out of place in contrast to the masculine power of those hands.

She wished suddenly she was not in her oldest jeans, and a T-shirt with a rip under one armpit. She wished she had not been so quick to tell Brit to leave her hair alone when her sister had tried to style it. Still, she kept her face deliberately expressionless, and hated herself for the weakness of wishing.

His attention, thankfully, wavered from her before her discomfort made her blurt out something she was sure to regret. An overreaction like *get the hell off my property.*

He cocked his head a little, turned a shoulder, listened. "You expecting company?"

"The movers," she said, suddenly hearing what he heard, the growl of a big truck coming down her rutted driveway.

"I expect they're here, then. I'll leave you to it—" he paused, leaving a blank where she could fill in her name, but she refused. She had no intention of appearing even remotely friendly to the handsome neighbor who had his eye on her land.

And, she realized, her lips.

Stunned by the pure masculine potency that burned briefly in his eyes when they flicked ever so briefly to her lips, she found herself wanting to sway toward him. Thankfully, he had tamed the heat in his gaze when he looked placidly back into her eyes.

She narrowed her eyes and glared at him.

He raised a hand to the brim of his hat, gave it a slow tip, and took a step backward onto the porch, turning away from her. "Your livestock appears to have arrived."

Her *what?* She scurried over to the doorway. He was planted on the top step now, his eyes narrowed at the old muffler-free truck that was bouncing down her drive, a stock rack in the back.

"I don't have any livestock."

He looked over his shoulder at her. In the full light he was even more compelling than he had been in the dimness of the cabin. The sunlight made him appear bigger and stronger and more real.

Dark brown hair that curled at the tips slipped out from under his cowboy hat and touched the nape of his neck.

She could see his pulse beating in the curve of that strong neck. The white T-shirt molded the firm, hard lines of his chest and the broad sweep of his shoulders. Where the short sleeve of the shirt ended a rock-cut bicep began. The white of the shirt made the copper tone of his skin appear deeper. Her eyes wandered down the length of that arm, to the corded muscle of a powerful forearm, the squareness of a wrist twice the width of her own.

Embarrassed for looking, she forced her gaze back up to his eyes.

She could see they were more than brown; they were dark as new-turned earth, flecked with little spangles of gold.

And in the strong sunlight, she could see those eyes held a pain in them that could compete with any of her own.

The truck pulled up at the bottom of her stairs, a vehicle in a state of disrepair worse than her Jeep.

Her neighbor stepped over her broken step with the ease of a man who was used to putting his feet in all the right places, and went up to the window, which the driver rolled down.

"Corrie Parsons?" The driver looked grizzled, and dirty. There was a look in his eyes that she could recognize at ninety yards. Plain old garden variety meanness.

Donahue looked back at her for confirmation, and she

nodded, not even sorry to give up her name to him after all. In fact she was glad suddenly that he was here. She got a familiar uneasy feeling from that man in the truck, with his stained teeth and squinty eyes and stubbled jowls.

With surprise she realized that Matt Donahue had either picked up on her split second of dislike, or harbored some of his own, because there was something almost protective in the way he turned back to the truck, and answered for her.

"This is the Parsons's place."

No one had ever protected her before, not even casually, and she did not like the way his small gesture threatened to soften something hard within her.

At that moment, a sound like Corrine had never heard reverberated through the air. It was like amplified finger-nails across a blackboard crossed with the shrill howl of a saw blade shrieking through wood.

Matt Donahue didn't jump back the way she did. In-stead, he moved away from the vehicle door, swung him-self up on the deck of the truck, and peered through the worn board slats of the stock rack.

"Yup," the man said, opening his door and sliding out, "I'm Werner Grimes, delivering a prize-winning mam-moth jack and he's all yours."

Matt Donahue jumped back down, shot a look over his shoulder at her that was distinctly grim.

"I thought you said you didn't have any livestock," Donahue said.

"I don't! I don't even know what a mammoth jack is. It sounds like something that's been extinct for several million years crossed with a rabbit."

"Ha-ha. That's 'bout as good a description of him as I've ever heard," Grimes said, going around to the back of his truck and lowering a ramp. "Mister, you want to give me a hand with this?"

"She says it's not hers."

"And this paper right here says it is, bought and paid for."

While the men were at the back of the truck, arguing ownership, she crept down the stairs of the cabin and came around to the side of the truck. She couldn't see anything. She climbed up on the deck, as she'd seen Matt do, only with less grace. She looked through the slats.

The saddest pair of brown eyes she had ever seen looked back at her from under bushy eyebrows. Long scruffy ears were turned toward the men, listening. For a moment it almost seemed like maybe it *was* some sort of prehistoric creature crossed with a rabbit.

"A donkey," she whispered. She stuck her finger through the slats and felt a soft, velvety nose touch her.

"Git your hand out of there!" the man shouted at her, and she jerked back so quickly she nearly fell off the wheel well. "Darned critter is meaner than a rattlesnake. He'll take off your arm at the elbow."

She stared at Grimes, aghast, and thought of the soft muzzle that had momentarily touched her fingers.

"Look, there's obviously been a mistake," her neighbor said.

"No mistake," Grimes insisted. "Right name. Right address. Stand back. I'm going to open the gate."

"She doesn't want a jack. And neither do I. I've got a pasture of full-blooded quarter horse mares right next door just foaling out, and I'll be damned if I'm planning a cross of mules next year."

"You better have a strong fence up then." The man spat. "He's hornier than—"

Donahue cut a look to her falling-down fences, and then

nterrupted Grimes before he had a chance to educate them
bout exactly how horny her donkey was.

Her donkey.

"How much to take him back wherever he came from?"

Her neighbor was reaching into his back pocket, taking
ut his wallet, which seemed to her to be a slightly auto-
ratic thing for him to be doing, though it was a little late
) decide she wanted control of the situation.

A certain whiney note appeared in the donkey-
eliverer's voice. "Geez. It took me near three hours to
)ad the sum-bit—"

"Just name a price," Donahue said coldly.

"Two hundred and fifty?"

"Get real."

"Okay. One fifty then. Not a penny less."

"I'll give you fifty bucks to turn that truck around, with
ne donkey onboard."

He was a mean donkey, Corrine reminded herself. He'd
ike her arm off at the elbow if she gave him the oppor-
unity. And apparently he had an immense appetite for
nings other than grass. A mean, disgusting donkey.

Whose muzzle had felt like velvet against her fingers.

And whose eyes had been so unbearably sad.

"Wait," she said, when she saw the money about to
hange hands. "Wait. I want him."

Something pitiful flashed in the donkey man's eyes as
e saw his chance to make a quick fifty bucks disappear-
ng.

Matt Donahue turned and looked at her. "You want
ho?"

Since only Donahue, Grimes and the donkey were in
er yard, her answer was bound to be insulting. Yet it gave
er great pleasure to say, "The donkey."

He came toward her in long strides, his eyes flashing

fire. "Do you have any idea what my brood stock i
worth?"

She shook her head, having only the vaguest idea wha
ever stock he was talking about was probably not regis
tered on the NASDAQ.

"One of my mares is worth more than this whole place
One mare."

She felt herself stiffen under the slight. She turned t
the other man. "Unload my donkey," she ordered.

"Yes, ma'am," he said glumly.

"Do you know anything about donkeys?" her neighbo
asked her.

"No," she said proudly. "But I bet they eat grass an
I have plenty of that."

"At the moment you don't have a fence that could hol
that beast."

She resented her donkey being called a beast in that ton
of voice. "Unload my donkey," she said again, her teet
clenched.

The man gave Matt a look that begged for his help, bu
he was ignored. Apparently Mr. Donahue's neighborlines
did not extend to unloading unwanted donkeys.

Cautiously Grimes walked up the ramp and inched bac
the gate of his stock rack.

The donkey made a whuffling noise.

"Easy there," Grimes said roughly.

She could hear the fear in his voice. What on earth wa
she doing? She was having a man unload a donkey in he
yard that *he* was afraid of. It was obviously some kind c
mistake that the donkey had been delivered here. Wh
make it worse by having him unloaded?

Was it the grim set of her neighbor's jaw that kept he
stubbornly, from calling out to Grimes to never mind? T
take the donkey and his fifty bucks and leave? Or was

the meanness in Grimes's eyes that made her reluctant to leave the donkey's fate up to him? Whatever the reason, she remained silent.

There was a loud scuffle, punctuated with swear words. And then, a shriek of pain, the sound of a heavy body falling, and the unmistakable thunder of hooves across the bed of the truck.

Matt leapt forward as the donkey burst from the truck and hurled himself down the ramp, kicking up his heels at his delighted and unexpected freedom.

It was short-lived. Matt grabbed the trailing rope and was dragged halfway across the yard skidding on his chest before he managed to get his legs back underneath him, and dig in his heels. His every muscle taut, he braced himself and used his entire body to force the donkey, fighting and kicking, around.

They moved in a circle, Donahue at the center of it, the heels of his boots planted in the ground, the muscles in his well-honed body rippling with the effort of trying to control the donkey who tore at the rope in his hands.

And then, just like that, the donkey quit, and stood there, his head sagging, his ribs heaving, his belly oddly huge in light of his pathetically thin body.

Even she, with no knowledge of any kind of livestock, could read a terrible story in that donkey's condition. His fur was matted. In places, there was no fur, only welts. He looked thin to the point of starvation, his hip bones sticking out. His mane and tail were barely visible for the burrs embedded in them.

Grimes had pulled himself up from the truck deck. He had a club in his hand, and a look in his eye, and Corrine yelped with wordless dismay as he moved toward the donkey.

Matt turned toward her sound, and saw the man coming toward him.

"You touch this animal," he said, his voice a low growl like a bear about to charge, "and I'll take that club to you."

She shivered at the pure menace Matt managed to exude without even raising his voice.

Grimes stopped, and eyed Donahue warily.

"Look at this poor dumb beast," Matt said, "He's been beaten. He's starving. His feet haven't been looked after. He's got worm belly." There was barely leashed fury in each carefully bitten out word.

Grimes was beating a hasty retreat to his truck. "He weren't never mine," he called over his shoulder as he climbed in his truck and slammed the door. "I just got paid to deliver him."

After two or three desperate grinding tries on the starter, the truck finally sputtered to life. It bounced back down the driveway at least twice as fast as it had come in.

Donahue did not turn and look back at her. "The kindest thing to do," he said, "would be to put him down."

The ice edge was gone from his voice, but it didn't make the message any less brutal.

"Kill him?" she breathed. A shudder went through her at the thought of the donkey being murdered. She didn't even want to think *how* one murdered a donkey, let alone the kind of person who could suggest such a thing. "No."

"He isn't trained," His voice was soft, almost gentle, a voice one might use on a stubborn child. "He doesn't look healthy. He seems to have a mean streak. The kindest thing to do—"

"Somehow kindness and cold-blooded murder don't go together in my world."

He sighed. The sigh whispered with the exasperation of

a country man facing a city girl, a man used to dealing with the hard cold realities of livestock coming face-to-face with a woman whose unrealistic love of all creatures great and small was probably based on a solid dose of Disney movies.

And even if she knew it was unrealistic, she wasn't letting him kill her donkey for the flimsy reason that the animal wasn't perfect.

After a long time, he spoke again. "Don't you have any idea where he came from? Or why he came to you?"

"No."

He glanced over his shoulder at her again, and sighed, the sigh even more heartfelt than his first one, if that were possible. "Then where do you want him, Ms. Parsons? And don't say your pasture until you've got your fences fixed, because you're legally libel for anything that happens to my mares."

Aha. The real reason he wanted her donkey dead.

"There's a stall in the barn."

"I'll put him in there for now. Tomorrow, I'll come look after the fences."

"I can look after my own fences."

"Humor me."

The donkey chose that moment to lunge at him, his teeth bared. Donahue sidestepped easily, shook his head and dragged the unwilling donkey toward her barn. She started to follow.

"Don't get too close behind him. He'd probably kick you as soon as look at you."

So, she trailed behind at a safe distance, and followed them into the murky barn. "I hope the barn doesn't fall down on top of him," she said, watching Donahue struggle with a rusted latch on a stall gate.

He gave her a look that said he hoped it did. He installed the donkey in the pen, stepped back and relatched the gate.

"Do you have any feed for him?"

She contemplated that for a moment. Feed for him. A hint might have been nice. Couldn't she just go pick some of that grass and throw it in here? Donahue read her mind.

"You don't even know what he eats, do you?" he asked, the softness of his tone not even beginning to hide his impatience.

"I'll go to the library and find out," she said proudly.

"That sounds a lot easier than just asking," he said sardonically.

She fought with her pride briefly then gave in with ill grace. "Okay. What does he eat?"

"He'll need hay, until you can get him on the grass. A couple of bales. And if you plan to build him up, he should probably have oats. Though," he frowned, "that might make him all the more eager to get after my mares."

"All right. I'll go get a couple of bales of hay, then, and some oats."

He glanced at his watch, and sighed. "Well, not today you won't. Feed store closed at five. You couldn't get hay there, anyway. You don't generally buy hay by the bale. You buy it by the ton."

The donkey let out an outraged bray that made the walls shake and made her worry the barn was going to come down around them.

"He'll need water right away. Don't go in there with him, you hear?"

The donkey chose that moment to lunge at the gate, so she decided not to argue with Donahue on the issue of entering the pen, even though she did not like the bossy tone of that *you hear?* She nodded stiffly.

"I'll bring by some straw for his bedding and enough

hay to get you through a few days until I can have a look at those fences.'' He glanced at his watch, and she caught a glimpse of weariness as he tried to figure out where to fit her into his day. ''I'll try to come around by eight or nine.''

She wanted desperately to tell him that wasn't necessary, that she would look after it herself. But the truth was, it was necessary. Her donkey could not wait on a point of pride. He looked like he might perish if he did not get the right kind of attention soon.

She didn't know a single soul who would know the first thing about giving a donkey the proper kind of care. Certainly her sisters would not. And their husbands were a lawyer and an ex-cop. Somehow that seemed far removed from donkey land.

''I'll pay you,'' she said proudly.

''Whatever.'' He stood regarding her for a moment, and then with a small shake of his head, he strode by her and was gone.

His scent lingered in her nostrils for a long, long time.

She went and put her hand cautiously over the gate to the stall, hoping the donkey would touch her fingers again with his muzzle and prove to her she had done the right thing.

But the donkey rolled his eyes at her, and stayed squished as tight against the back wall of his new home as he could go.

''I know all about that feeling,'' she said, and she smiled, knowing she had done just the right thing after all.

Chapter Two

"**M**r. Donahue, you're late. You know we have fines for people who pick up their children late."

"Yeah, yeah. Put it on my bill. Would you tell my nephew I'm here?"

That irritating woman, Mrs. Beatle, was actually wagging her finger at *him*. Not as easily intimidated by a certain tone of voice, a set of jaw, as Grimes had been.

He sighed. "Please?"

Townspeople just never got it. Mares foaled. Colts in training went berserk. Donkeys arrived. You couldn't just drop everything and run to town because it was five-thirty precisely and the day care was closing.

He had days, usually in the spring when mares were foaling and he was operating on two or three hours sleep a night, when he dreamed of a job that quit at five-thirty. Or six-thirty. Or ten-thirty. Or midnight.

On the other hand, a man traded something for a job like that. Freedom. He had never addressed another man as his boss, and he was not sure that he ever could.

"Robbie," he called. Mrs. Beatle was hellbent on continuing her lecture on punctuality, as if he was a ten-year-old boy and not a man who was tough as nails from wrangling horses for a living.

What was it today? He'd put out a magnet for difficult women?

Not that Mrs. Beatle was in the same category as *her*. His new neighbor. Not even close. Mrs. Beatle was old and gray and built like a refrigerator.

Where as the new neighbor was young and not gray and not built anything like a refrigerator. It occurred to him it had been a long time since anything had gotten his attention quite as completely as she had.

In his mind's eye he could see her, startling like a deer, when he'd first walked in the door. A rude thing for him to do, but the door had been open, and it was hard to think of that falling down cabin as belonging to anyone but him. The property had been in his family for several generations.

Until he'd sold it. It still felt like some kind of failure that he'd sold off that parcel of land. Maybe that's why he wanted it back so badly. As if he could erase a whole bad period of his life by erasing the evidence.

At first glance, in that dimly lit cabin, his new neighbor had looked like a teenager. She'd been wearing jeans that were too small, and a T-shirt that was too large. Her hair had looked like a candle flame, yellow, dancing with light, pulled back into a ponytail like the cheerleaders at Miracle Harbor High used to wear.

Except unlike the cheerleaders, who'd always worn those vaguely irritating wholesome expressions of good cheer, in that first second, before she masked it, Corrine Parsons had looked scared damned near to death.

He'd seen right away the fear wasn't caused by him,

even if he had startled her. It was something she carried deep inside her.

He wondered what put that kind of fear into a person. She had denied the fear, but he knew what he had seen. He worked with fear all the time. Skittish two-year-olds, green colts, horses other people had given up on.

Back when he'd focused more on training than breeding, he used to specialize in horses like that. Maybe he was just irresistibly attracted to frightened things.

Sometimes those horses were just scared because they didn't know what you expected from them. Sometimes they had nervous natures. But other times, the fear had been put there.

Those were the ones who broke your heart. The ones whose trust had been shattered.

Her mammoth jack being a prime example. The animal wasn't mean. It was scared out of its wits. Matt felt sick with helpless fury when he remembered the condition that animal had been in. Still, an animal with that kind of fear was the most dangerous kind of all. It always felt it was fighting for its life, and it was a nearly impossible chore to convince it of anything differently.

He felt a strange little fissure of pain when he thought of her fear in that same light. He didn't think Corrine Parsons was crabby by nature, like Mrs. Beatle here, who was on chapter two of her lecture on being responsible as an example to his nephew. He suspected, somehow and somewhere along the line, that Corrie Parsons had come to believe she was fighting for her life.

There was no meanness in her eyes. Her eyes had been soft and scared and pretty as those Striped Beauty crocuses his sister had planted along his front walk, along with a bunch of other flowers, about a million years ago.

"They're signs of hope," Marianne had said firmly, back when they all still had some of that.

Still, if that kind of fear was dangerous in an animal, it would be more so in a woman.

And if an animal could break his heart...

He reminded himself, firmly, that his heart was pretty much already in pieces. He wasn't taking any more chances with it.

Nope, his complicated, beautiful neighbor would be a good woman to stay away from.

She was a city girl, anyway. It was written all over her— the milky skin on her face, the creamy softness of hands with no rings on them. It had been written all over her even before the donkey showed up.

She might be able to handle that cabin in the spring and summer, but in a few months the cold, wet weather would settle in and icy winds would begin to blow in off the ocean. Her driveway would turn to soup, and she would have to chop wood to keep warm. That would be it for her. Maybe even before that, if he had the good luck to have a skunk cozy up underneath the floorboards of the cabin. It wouldn't be the first time.

Real estate had a tendency to lose value when strong scents attached themselves to it. He could probably get the land for a song.

Unfortunately, he had already registered the soft curves of a slender body, the plump swell of her lower lip. Unfortunately, he had already felt a little twinge of that *something* that could do in the strongest of men.

Desire.

It wouldn't just be a good idea to stay away from her until she called it quits voluntarily. It was imperative.

Imperative, he repeated to a mind that wasn't all together in agreement with him.

And unfortunately, he'd tangled himself with her for a little bit. He wondered if she'd consider castrating the donkey. It would save him one hell of a pile of work on those fences.

Of course, after her reaction to his perfectly reasonable suggestion they *murder* her donkey, she'd probably rather castrate Matt Donahue.

He heard Robbie coming before he saw him, small feet flying along tiled floors. And then Robbie rounded a corner and skidded to a halt, and Matt smiled.

His first smile since meeting the new neighbor. And her donkey.

Robbie was five. His nephew. He was as fair as Matt was dark, his blond hair the same color as corn tassels, his blue eyes huge, the exact color of sapphires. He looked so much like his mother had looked at that age, that Matt could rarely see him without feeling the catch in his throat.

His smile faded and he recognized the sadness that felt like it would never go away.

How could a woman of twenty-seven die of breast cancer? A woman who had been the sole parent to her child? His sister, Marianne, had had the laughter and life sucked out of her until she was wasted, so wracked with pain it had been a mercy when she died.

He shook his head, trying to be free of the anger and sadness and bewilderment that mingled in him, and that he saw mirrored in his tiny nephew.

Until he'd put his younger sister in the ground, Matt had had a faith of sorts. Not a church-going kind of faith, but a kind of simple reverence for the miracle of a new foal, an awe at the hardiness of spring flowers, a kind of un-stated belief that in the end good generally won.

Now, he felt like a man who had been through a war, not at all certain what he believed about anything anymore.

He went down on his haunches and held open his arms. Robbie catapulted into him, and he pretended to be knocked over. Under Mrs. Beatle's disapproving eye, he and his nephew wrestled across the floor. He didn't stop until Robbie was shouting with laughter.

"Are we going to see Robbie tomorrow, Mr. Donahue?" Mrs. Beatle asked tightly, when they had both picked themselves up off the floor.

Robbie's hand tightened on his, and Matt looked down into those imploring eyes. Everyone said day care was good for his nephew. They said it wasn't good for him to trail his uncle around the horse operation like a tiny shadow. They said he needed to socialize with kids his own age, that he needed to learn to count, and that did not include measuring horse rations. They said he should be watching *Sesame Street*, not the stallion on the mares, or the mares having foals. They said Robbie's life needed to have structure.

So he could learn to pick up his kid promptly at five someday, Matt thought testily.

Besides, how could you inflict Mrs. Beatle on someone you loved two days in a row?

And he loved Robbie. In fact, the boy's presence in his life had Matt discovering the oddest tender regions in a heart he had always foolishly assumed was as tough as the rest of him. He had never felt anything like the feeling that boy put in his heart. And maybe that was a little something worth believing in, when he could find nothing else.

His sister had told him the love would survive.

He clung to that some days, that one truth.

"Uh, no, Mrs. Beatle, he won't be coming tomorrow."

"Ms. Bettle," Robbie corrected him in a loud whisper, and then beamed at him.

Ms. Bettle—what kind of fool would marry her after

all—made a sucking sound with her lips. Ignoring her, Matt hoisted his nephew onto his shoulders, ducked under the doorway and went out into the bright May sunshine.

"Auntie, I'm hungry."

Auntie. No amount of begging or pleading or ordering or demanding could change it. Robbie's first attempts at Matt, had come out Auntie, and he stubbornly refused to budge on this issue. His uncle was *Auntie,* period. In a small town, it was like being a boy named Sue, a cross Matt bore better on some days than others.

The kid was always hungry. Matt tried to think what he had for groceries in that lonely house he and Robbie now shared.

Macaroni and cheese, but they'd had that last night. Wieners and beans, but they'd had that the night before. Taco chips and Cheez Whiz spread, but that didn't count as real food for some reason. Somewhere in his limited inventory of kid information he knew he was supposed to be feeding Robbie at least some stuff that was green.

"You want to go for a hamburger?" At least that would have Walt's big, fat homemade pickle on the side. Green.

Robbie nodded happily.

Maybe if Matt ordered a salad, too, even though neither of them would eat it, he wouldn't feel so bloody guilty about his absolute failure in the nutritional health department.

He wondered if *she* knew anything about nutritional health, and was annoyed with himself for wondering.

He didn't have to wonder for long. After he and Robbie had eaten, he went home, fed his own horses, then loaded a few bales, and returned to her place. She was sitting on her front step eating a bag of potato chips. Her furniture, and boxes, were stacked on the porch all around her.

He looked sternly at his nephew. "Stay here. I'll only

be a second.'' The astonishing truth was he didn't want Robbie calling him auntie in front of her. He got out of the truck.

She rose to greet him, slender, innately graceful. She wiped her hands on the seat of her jeans, which he really wished she hadn't done. How could she be slender and curvy at the same damned time?

"Supper?" he guessed, a lame conversation opener, not that he wanted a conversation, despite the intriguing sight of her behind. He just wanted to dump his bales and go home.

After reading Robbie that book his nephew loved a couple of times, he could go to bed.

She gave him a look that told him her supper was none of his business, then offered grudgingly, "I'm trying to get the inside cleaned up before I put my stuff in."

Robbie, obedient only when it was convenient, as always, finally managed to get himself out the passenger side of the truck. He came around and stood gazing at her. "I'm Robbie," he announced, finally.

"Hi, Robbie," she said, not moving on to any of that sentimental gushing that made Matt just cringe. Robbie wasn't too fond of it either. "I'm Corrine. You can call me Corrie."

"My nephew," Matt said, and then as way of a hint to Robbie, "I'm his *uncle*."

She gave him a sour look that said she had figured that out. If she was any pricklier, roses would be growing out of the top of her head.

"How old are you, Corrie?" Robbie asked, missing the prickliness apparently.

"Twenty-seven," she said, without apology or giggling or even flinching.

Finally, something he liked about her, Matt thought,

then realized how bloody tired he was. He'd been up since five-thirty, and suddenly he knew he was not up to this, to standing around making small talk with a woman who seemed to have grown less likable and more gorgeous since this afternoon.

Maybe because some of that honey-gold hair had fallen free from the ponytail. But the evening light had not softened the unfriendliness of her, though he reluctantly noticed she did not look so scared anymore. Just untouchable. And tired, like him.

"I'm five," Robbie said, a conversation opener that had to be cut off quick.

Matt brought it back to business. "I brought you a couple of bales and a sack of oats for your donkey."

Leave it at that, an inner voice advised him. Besides, she looked like she'd rather kill him than owe him anything. But he couldn't. The welfare of the animal came before his desire not to get frost-burn from the ice queen.

"He'll need to be wormed, and have his feet trimmed soon, too. I don't think I could do it without throwing him."

"Donkey?" Robbie breathed.

Half a million dollars of horse flesh at home that he couldn't persuade his nephew to be even mildly interested in, but the word *donkey* was said in the same tone usually reserved for The Rock, Robbie's favorite wrestler.

"Ms. Parsons has a donkey," Matt offered reluctantly.

"I *love* donkeys," Robbie declared firmly.

"Since when?" Matt snapped, then turned back to her before this got out of hand, "Look, since you probably don't want me to throw your donkey—"

"Even you can't throw a donkey," Robbie decided solemnly.

"I don't know what that means," she added uneasily, "throwing him."

"It means roping his feet, yanking them out from under him." Was he deliberately making himself sound like a barbarian? If so, it was working. His nephew and his neighbor were both looking at him with horror.

"And since you probably don't want me to do that," he continued, "and since his feet and his worms are going to have to be looked after, you probably want to get a vet up here. Soon."

"How soon?" she said. "I mean, I think he's been traumatized enough for now."

He contemplated that. A donkey *traumatized*. A tiny puncture in her armor, and it was for a donkey.

"I'll give you the name of a good vet. She can come out and do it for you. She'll give him a sedative if he's too difficult to work with." He knew he'd feel guilty if he told her what it would cost, because the bottom of her jeans were worn nearly plum through, and she was driving a jeep that had probably done service in the Second World War.

Still, if she was going to go to the trouble of having the vet all the way out here for that flea-bitten varmint, she might as well kill two birds with one stone. Or two balls with one scalpel, whatever the case might be.

"And while she's here," he said, his tone so neutral as to appear casual, "you might want to have her castrate him."

"Castrate?" He'd been around women just enough to know arms folded over the chest like that were not a good sign.

"It would be the kindest thing." He said it with the full authority of a man who had spent his entire life around livestock. His tone was as convincing as he could make it.

"Right after murder," she snapped back, unconvinced.

"It would improve his temperament." He heard just a little note of irritation in his own voice. He tried to think if he'd ever struck out quite this thoroughly with a woman.

A dangerous little sparkle had appeared in her eyes. "And of course, if he were castrated he wouldn't be after your mares."

"Gee, I hadn't thought of that." He said this with as much innocence as he could muster, but she wasn't fooled.

Come to think of it, in order to strike out, he'd have to *want* to run the bases. Tangling with a porcupine would be about twice the fun as tangling with her. In any sense of the word.

"What's catrated mean?" Robbie asked innocently.

She looked smug, and he had the uneasy feeling she and Robbie had somehow just become conspirators against him.

"I'll tell you later."

"I want to know now."

"No."

Robbie looked stunned. Matt had never taken that tone with him, and somehow it felt like it was all her fault that he had now.

"Can I go see the donkey?" Robbie asked in a small voice. "Oh, please, Auntie? Please?"

"Auntie?" she said, incredulous.

Matt sighed. There. At least he didn't have to worry about his secret name getting out anymore. It was not as if she liked him, anyway. Big surprise that the first hint of a smile from her was at his expense.

It was not as if he *cared* if she liked him.

"You know what? It's a long story, and I'm not in the mood for telling it. Could I just dump the hay, introduce my kid to your donkey and go home?"

"Certainly," she said, as if she couldn't think of anying she wanted more than for his stay to be a brief one, o.

"Great, hop in the truck."

She didn't unfold her arms from her chest.

"You want to know how to feed him, right?"

She glared at Matt for a moment, and then with ill grace opped on the tailgate of the truck. Not in the cab. He noked back his desire to tell her he hadn't bitten anyone ecently. To his annoyance, Robbie-turn-coat, jumped on ne tailgate with her.

In the rearview mirror he saw her tuck some of that rayward hair behind her ears, adjust her T-shirt, and lick er lips. He ordered himself not to wonder if that meant nything.

Did that mean anything?

"I sure as hell hope not," he said out loud.

He backed his truck up to the barn, and by the time he vent around the back, she was trying her darndest to heft ne of the bales out of there.

Seventy pounds. She had both hands inserted between ne twine and the hay. She lifted. Nothing happened.

He knew damn well what the twine would do to soft ands, but she didn't quit. With a mighty grunt she picked ne hay up three inches, moved forward one, and dropped

"I'll get it."

He might as well have saved his breath, because she ave him a look of fierce pride, squatted down and shoved ne bale with her shoulder. It moved another millimeter or o. It would be fun to cross his arms and watch, but that asn't the kind of boy his mama had raised.

He climbed in the truck bed, moved carefully around er, and tossed down the other two bales, which also

earned him a glare. Was he supposed to apologize for th
fact he was a man? That some things that came hard t
her, came easy to him?

He wondered what would happen if he told her sh
looked like a Sumo wrestler.

That would be the end of hair-tucking and lip-licking.

Still, he didn't tell her. Because it wasn't precisely true
The position yes, but the beauty? She looked more breath
taking than ever with her little pink tongue poking ou
between her teeth, and her face flushed red, and the swea
beginning to pop out on her brow.

Pretending to ignore her, he moved back around her
hopped off the truck, picked up his two bales, one in eacl
hand, and went into the barn.

Now you're showing off, an annoying little voice insid
his head informed him.

Showing off? What for? He'd already decided she wa
pure poison.

He glanced over his shoulder. She had managed to tum
ble her bale off the back of the truck. Now she and Robbi
were rolling it laboriously toward the barn.

Panting, with a final grunt, she finally managed to ge
it in the door.

Pretending she didn't have his full attention, he slippe
his pocket knife from his back pocket and cut the twine.

She came and watched.

Her bosom was heaving nicely under her too large shir

"See how the hay breaks apart?" he asked. "That"
called a flake." He explained to her, carefully, how to fee
the donkey, the repercussions if it wasn't done right.

There. He sounded like a reasonable man. A man whos
mind was a million miles away from heaving bosoms. Re
ally, it was one of the rotten parts of being a man. Natur

oticing whatever the hell it wanted to notice, even when e'd already told his mind, *no way, never, forget it.*

He turned swiftly away from her and shook the first two akes out into the hay crib. The donkey thanked him by attening his floppy ears to his ugly head and charging the ence. Robbie oohed and aahed as if he was seeing an nimal that was both lovable and exotic. She was also miling indulgently at the donkey's exceedingly bad man-ers.

Just above the barn smells, the fresh hay, and the don-ey, he could smell her. Her shampoo, and her soap and er deodorant, and something else so sweet and soft it near ook his breath away. Matt tried to place the scent and ouldn't.

What he could do was never come back here again. ver.

Of course, if he chose that, he was going to have a crop f little mules running around next year, after that donkey ushed down the fences and bred all his mares. He could hange the name of his pure-breed quarter horse ranch rom No Quarter Asked, to No Quarter Assed.

"Auntie," Robbie announced sleepily, tucking his head gainst Matt's belly as they headed for home a few ninutes later, "I'm coming to see that donkey again real oon."

Somehow it didn't even sound like a question, or a re-uest.

His nephew had just told him how it was going to be.

Life was telling him how it was going to be, but he still ught it.

"Don't you think your own horse is better?" he sug-ested subtly. "You can ride her. Pet her. Get close to er."

"I don't like Cupie Doll," Robbie announced firmly
"She has real mean eyes."

Cupie Doll was a prizewinning brood mare that Matt
had reluctantly retired. She wouldn't take anymore. And
Robbie, unfortunately was right. Sweet as shortcake when
she was pregnant, she seemed miserable when she was not
growing fat with a baby.

As a riding horse she was a gem. Gentle. Predictable
A perfect mount for a child. But the sullen expression
hadn't left her face since her last heat had come and gone
without her seeing any action.

Maybe Robbie noticed more about the horses than Matt
had given him credit for.

"And that *thing* back there doesn't have mean eyes?"
Matt sputtered.

"Corrie?" Robbie asked, indignant.

Even Matt couldn't make himself go that far. For all the
bristle of her personality, there was no meanness in her
eyes. "The donkey," he said.

"Oh, no. He doesn't have mean eyes. Can I go back
Please, Auntie?"

It was the first real enthusiasm he'd seen Robbie show
for anything in a long, long time. The pair of them had
been walking around in a daze since Marianne died.

Six months ago, already.

What was it about that donkey that so appealed to his
nephew? Maybe being attracted to frightened things ran in
the family.

Whatever it was, he couldn't put out the light in his
nephew's eyes. Not even for his own self-preservation.

"We'll go back in a few days." He figured he'd left her
over a week's supply of grub for the donkey. He had to
go look after those fences, anyway.

"Okay," Robbie agreed with a yawn. "She's a pretty lady. I like her eyes. Lots of colors."

"Really." He did not say this with anything approaching encouragement. He certainly did not let on that he had already committed the offense of comparing her eyes to crocuses.

Lots of colors. He'd have to have another look when he went back over there and tried to set up a fence that would hold a determined donkey back.

The fence that needed to go up, was the one around a mind that rebelliously wanted to recall her heaving bosom and delicate scent.

Matt sighed. This was not the first time life had been wrested from his control. It just seemed that every time it happened, he could count on a bad ending.

Corrine watched his truck pull away. It wasn't until it was out of her driveway that she allowed herself to breathe again.

What was it about a man's easy strength that made a woman go weak with longing?

When he'd hefted those bales, one in each hand, she'd been resentful. But right underneath the resentment, something else flickered dangerously to life.

Desire.

"Corrie Parsons," she informed herself, doing one last check of the donkey, who flattened his ears menacingly when she got too close to his grub, "you will not be ruled by something so base."

A little voice inside her whined piteously.

She ignored it, throwing herself into finishing cleaning the cabin.

Finally, exhausted, she dragged a mattress in, and flopped on it in the middle of her living room floor.

But her plan, to work herself to exhaustion so she couldn't think of anything else, had backfired.

She was too exhausted to control her thoughts at all.

And her thoughts drifted to Matt Donahue as naturally as waves drift to shore. She pictured him lifting those bales, one in each hand, the coil of the muscle in his arms, the faint gleam of sweat on the back of his neck.

She remembered, with perfect clarity the look in his eyes, that calm, quiet look that seemed to be taking in far more than she wanted to reveal.

She tried to get herself under control by reminding herself that he was after all, the man who spoke so carelessly of a donkey's demise, who had suggested castration.

Instead, she pictured the look on his face when his nephew had called him Auntie, and laughed softly to herself.

So big, so masculine, so strong, and cool. Auntie.

Her mind drifted to his nephew.

The truth was, despite the success of her *Brandy* book, Corrine didn't like children one-on-one and face-to-face. That was why she never did readings. Children were far too vulnerable. Too wide open. Too willing to trust and to love.

Children required something of her that she was not able to give.

She sighed. The donkey began to bray and wouldn't stop, his mournful *ee-haws* scraping across the silent night.

It struck her suddenly. She had let that man take care of her. She'd let him take over, was more like it.

Okay. Today had been an emergency of sorts because of the unexpected arrival of the donkey. But if she let him back over to fix those fences, that was something else.

She was precariously close to being needy.

Humor me, he'd said in that deep, authoritative drawl when she'd told him she could fix her own fences.

That was infuriating! As if she couldn't be responsible for a donkey! As if she couldn't fix a fence!

She was determined, now, to scorn his offers of help. There was something about him that was far too dangerous to her. She would finish the work necessary to keep the donkey all by herself.

All by herself.

She knew from experience that was the safest way.

Chapter Three

He managed to hold off going back to her place for six days, the donkey's food supply and his ability to ward off his nephew's pleas to return, dwindling at precisely the same time.

It occurred to Matt that he might as well have given in and gone to his neighbor's every day. Maybe, had she had the daily opportunity, she would have succeeded in insulting him enough that in unguarded moments she wouldn't haunt his thoughts, the way she did now.

For some reason, it was her eyes he thought of, instead of her barbed tongue. And her lips, that moment when she had run her tongue nervously over them and made them glisten as if they'd been touched by morning dew.

Which just went to show a man could talk himself into just about anything if he'd gone too long without a kiss.

The fact that he couldn't even remember the last kiss of a passionate nature he had shared with a female was probably indication enough it had been too long. He frowned. Was Barbara the last woman he had kissed? They'd gone their separate ways shortly after his sister had been diagnosed. That was a hell of a long time. No wonder he was vulnerable.

With this vulnerability in mind, he arrived good and early. With any luck he'd have that fence slammed back up before she was even out of bed.

"You go look at the donkey, Robbie. And I'll go see if—" *the gorgeous witch* echoed through his mind and he paused.

"Corrie," Robbie filled in for him.

"Corrie," Matt agreed reluctantly, though he knew Ms. Parsons would be a whole lot safer, "...is up. Don't go in the pen with the donkey under any circumstances, you hear?"

Robbie nodded solemnly. "Okay, Auntie."

That particular cat was already out of the bag, so Matt pulled back his shoulders and went up her steps, remembering to hop the second one which was a leg-breaker if he had ever seen one. But even before he got to the top of the steps he heard the uneven staccato of a hammer.

He turned and squinted into the sun. There she was, a bright spot of color dressed as she was in a yellow shirt and standing out in the field in amongst all that grass.

Fixing that fence all by herself.

He knew, somehow, that would be a point of pride with her, and his sensible self told him to go collect Robbie from the donkey and get out of here.

The fact that he felt an unwanted little twinge of pity for her only underscored the wisdom of getting out of here and fast.

There was something sad about her thinking she had to do everything by herself, like she had something to prove.

Leave, he ordered himself.

But suddenly he felt like Marianne was watching him,

looking disappointed, waiting for him to do the gentle-manly thing, the neighborly thing, the right thing. Mari-anne had been a woman alone. What if it had been her out there, trying to fix her fence? What would he have thought of a man who turned his back on her, walked away?

He sighed, moved off the steps, and inspected what she had accomplished so far. He wondered if it had taken her six days to make this mess. Fallen two-by-six rails had been uniformly hung on the wrong side of the posts. They slanted up or down instead of running in a nice straight line. He studied a fresh nail suspiciously, tapped the board with the palm of his hand. The board broke away easily. As he suspected, she was using nails that were intended for hanging pictures.

Donkey-proof fences took a certain amount of expertise.

He went back to his truck, reached into the box and took out his tool apron. He strapped it on with a certain reluctance, wondering if this is what gladiators had felt like getting ready to go into the arena.

Robbie had planted himself on an overturned barrel and was chatting to the donkey, who was ignoring him.

"I'm going to be working down the fence right out there. You want to come? You can help." The magic words.

"No thanks. I'll stay here."

It was the first time his nephew had chosen not to do something with him, and Matt was slightly taken aback by it. Jealous of the damned donkey. He'd just known that donkey was bad news from the first moment he'd laid eyes on it.

Shaking his head, Matt went back out into the sunlight, and made his way down the fence of the paddock that adjoined the barn.

He made sure to make lots of noise as he approached

her, not wanting to startle her again. Besides, that gave her lots of time to paste that sour look on her face, a look that did not appreciate his being a gentleman, or a good neighbor, one little bit.

He should have run when he had the opportunity.

"Good morning," he said.

She was trying to hold one end of a downed two-by-six in place, high up the post, and hammer it at the same time. Once she got the first end fastened it should be easier, if her flimsy nails held. She glanced at him, as if she had not heard him coming, looked back to the fence.

"I'll look after my own fences, thanks," she gasped, took a mighty swing at her nail and missed completely.

She cast a swift look at him and he knew if he smiled he'd be in big trouble.

"It's a good fence," he said, looking off into the distance. "I built it the summer I was sixteen. Guess it's about time it started falling down in places." He graciously pretended he hadn't seen her miss. He took inventory. She was using what he referred to as a toy hammer. His sister had had one, too. For hanging pictures and such. "The boards are still in pretty good shape, all things considered."

Bang. Bang. Bang.

Casually, he lifted the other end of the board for her. She glared at him, but hammered her nail home.

"Generally," he said carefully, "when you're building this kind of fence, you mount the board on the inside of the post."

She stopped and stared at him, and he noticed Robbie had been right about her eyes. They were green and blue and brown and a whole lot of shades in between. Hazel didn't say the half of it. Then she slid a look back down the fence, at her whole line of boards mounted on the outside of the posts.

She gave him a haughty look—that branded him one of those know-it-all men who were always finding fault.

He knew he might as well get it over with. Drop the glove, so to speak. He walked over to where she had just driven the nail home. He could smell that same heady smell that was all hers. Her hair gleamed in the morning sunlight, and if he was not mistaken a freckle or two was dotting her nose.

She was wearing a button-up shirt today, yellow as a dandelion, and it suited her. Her jeans still were worn in all the wrong places—or the right ones, depending on how you looked at it. And who looked at it.

"You see," he said, "if an animal tries this fence," he rapped it softly with his hammer, a real hammer, a 16-ounce framing hammer, "it gives under the pressure."

The board fell away, and she gave a dismayed little squeak.

"But if you hammer it on this side, it holds. If something hits it, the nail doesn't pull free."

"Oh," she said ungraciously.

"Plus, you want to use a big nail. Three inches." He peered at the nail that had just pulled free of the wood. "What kind of nail is this?"

"I wasn't aware nails had names."

He carefully avoided the argument she was trying to walk him into. "And a big hammer makes driving the nails in easier."

"So, wrong side, wrong nails, wrong hammer. Am I doing anything right?"

"Uh, actually, no."

She looked like she was going to throw her hammer. At him.

"It'll only take me a few minutes to put it right," he said hastily, "if you want to do something else."

"Like make tea and bake cookies?" she said dangerously.

"Ma'am, I've been doing this kind of work my whole life. I'm not questioning your capabilities or trying to insult you. I'm just trying to keep your donkey away from my mares."

"You have that look on your face."

"What look?" he asked incredulously.

"That, *oh, isn't she cute, she's a woman with a hammer* look."

This was a no-win if he'd ever been in one. If he told her she wasn't cute he'd be in trouble, and if he agreed she was, he'd be in trouble, too.

He chose action. "I can show you how to do it."

"I don't need your help!"

"I can see that, but I hope you'll humor me. Those are my mares on the west side of your fence."

"And I'm libel if something happens to them," she remembered cynically.

He saw instantly she was having an easier time accepting his help on those terms—if it were about him, and not about her—and so he shrugged. It really was about his mares, wasn't it?

Or somewhere, walking down the fence line, seeing those pathetically hung planks, had it become about something else? Something even more than being the man Marianne would have expected him to be?

Something about chasing a little of that wariness from her eyes?

Don't even think it, he warned himself. He reached into his apron and handed her a fistful of real nails. "Be careful with these. Nails and hooves don't get along."

That made her send a panicked look down the way she had come, probably dropping nails the whole way.

"Robbie's at the barn with your donkey. Is that okay with you?" He picked up the plank. "You want to grab that end?"

"I've made quite a bit of progress with that donkey," she said, and did what he asked without protesting.

Don't ask, he told himself, but he did anyway. "What do you consider progress?"

"He doesn't hate me anymore."

Geez. Call out for the balloons and champagne. "That's nice," he said. He leaned over, closed one eye, and looked down the length of the plank. "Lift up your end a hair. A touch more. Right there. Nail it."

"Do you look after Robbie while his mom works?"

It occurred to him the question was a pretty close replica of conversation. He didn't know why it caught him up the side of the head. Maybe because this was a small town and everybody *knew*.

"My sister died," he said gruffly, turning deliberately away from her. He wanted to stop there. He ordered himself to stop there, but the words just kept coming out. "Breast cancer. She was only twenty-seven."

"Matt, that's so sad and terrible. I'm sorry."

He glanced at her, and the frigid look had melted from her face. Her eyes had gone huge and damp, and she had her bottom lip caught in between her teeth so hard he was surprised she didn't draw her own blood.

In a blinding flash of understanding, a piece of her puzzle fell neatly into place. She was one of those people who just felt everything too deeply. She'd put up a wall to protect herself from the intensity of her own feelings.

"When did it happen?" she asked softly. She had

moved beside him, and her hand found his sleeve, rested there on his arm.

And made him feel a few things a little too deeply, too. A need to talk. To tell. To let the pain pour out until it was gone.

He was stunned by how vulnerable she had made him feel with a single touch.

She seemed to realize suddenly she was touching him, because she pulled her hand away and stood looking at it with shocked dismay, as if it had betrayed her.

"It's been six months."

"Is Robbie okay?" she whispered.

"Most days."

She didn't ask if he was, thank God. Deliberately, he set to work. She caught on quickly. With both of them working, it only took a few seconds per post to switch the top rail to the opposite side.

"Where's his dad?" she asked after a little bit.

"My sister would never tell anyone who his father was," he answered simply. Then, because she'd started it, he felt asking her a question should be fair play. "What brings you to Miracle Harbor? What's your accent? It sounds Northern." He knew he was cheating a bit by asking two questions.

"I have family here," she said. "I'm from Minnesota."

The tone of her voice told him two things. Her family meant everything to her. And she didn't like answering questions about herself. He decided to try for one more, anyway. He'd always liked to live dangerously.

"What are you going to do here?"

"Provide a shelter for homeless donkeys," she said, deadpan, her wall back up.

It didn't really make sense. The question had been innocuous enough. But then nearly thirty years on the planet should have taught him at least that nothing about women made sense. Not the way they stirred up feelings inside you, even when they were being downright rude. Not the way your eyes drifted to lips that were tight with held-in emotion, and dreamed of what they would taste like.

His shoulders set in a straight line that would have defied anybody to guess he was trying to make sense of that which would not be made sense of, he turned away from her, slipped his hammer into the loop on his tool apron.

"I'm just going to go check on Robbie."

Robbie had not shifted position at all, and was still chatting happily to the donkey who was now snoozing, his weight on three feet, one resting, one ear back and one pointed right at Robbie.

Robbie hadn't seen Matt yet, and he paused in the doorway, listened.

"And my mom smelled like good things—cookies out of the oven and sheets out of the dryer."

Things, Matt thought regretfully, Robbie had not smelled for a long time. Robbie had not spoken to Matt about Marianne. Why? Did he see the pain in his uncle's eyes every time the name was mentioned? Had Matt unconsciously shut him down when he tried?

Or maybe the donkey was just safe. No answer back. No shared grief. Just long ears and closed eyes. The donkey really did look like he was listening wisely.

"Hi," Matt said softly.

Robbie turned and smiled at him, a real smile, that actually touched his eyes. "He's such a nice donkey," Robbie proclaimed softly.

The donkey snapped awake, proved how "nice" he was by laying his ears back at Matt, turning his rump to him and then looking over his shoulder and baring his long yellow teeth.

"Oh, yeah, I can see he's Mr. Congeniality, all right. You want to come help me with that fence now?"

But Robbie, who usually jumped at the opportunity to be of assistance, didn't even look at his uncle. "Oh, no. I'm in the middle of telling him some important things."

Could he say now *I'll listen to those important things?* What if he didn't know what to do with them once he heard them?

The donkey passed wind, and Robbie clapped with as much delighted approval as if the beast had whistled dixie.

"There's a soda in the cooler in the back of the truck if you want one," Matt said.

"'Kay."

He went and helped himself from that cooler, hesitated and then took one for her, and made his way back down the fence line.

"Ready for a break?" he asked her.

The sun was rising steadily now, with that burst of heat that sometimes came late in May.

She had sweat in her eyes and under her armpits.

"I really can manage the rest. I've got it figured out now."

"I know, but my nephew is romancing your donkey, and I'm not allowed to leave yet." He wanted to tell her his nephew was up there confiding in the donkey about his dead mother, and ask her if she knew what to do about that, especially in light of the reluctant smile that crossed her lips and turned her from plain pretty to just beautiful in the blink of an eye.

She eyed the soda with wanting. She deliberately turned away from it, hammered another nail, which bent over crooked at the second wallop.

If she could have said what she was really feeling, maybe he could have to, but he knew with scared things

the worst thing you could do was rush your fences. Not
that he was even entertaining a notion of taming her.

He'd settle for not frightening her anymore than she had
been already.

So, he popped the tab on the soda and handed it to her.

Resignedly, she put down her hammer, and took a swig.
He bet she wouldn't be able to find her hammer later.

He reached over with the claw of his own hammer, and
as unobtrusively as he could, he straightened her bent nail.
He hit it home in two slams.

You're showing off again, that little voice inside his
head taunted him.

And even though he was sure he hadn't been showing
off, he didn't miss the way her eyes fastened for a moment
on the muscle in his biceps, before she looked quickly
away.

He was going to be in over his head before he knew it
if he didn't watch out. On the other hand, watching out
was one of his specialties.

Corrine took another sip of her soda and berated herself.
She had been so sure of herself, fierce in her determination
not to accept his help, nothing personal.

Now, she had not only accepted his help, she was swig-
ging his soda and eyeing his biceps, an embarrassing fact
that he didn't seem to have missed.

But the little boy being his nephew and the death of his
sister seemed to change everything. That beautiful little
boy with his china-plate eyes and winsome smile missing
his mommy.

She was irresistibly attracted to orphans, she supposed.
That's why her *Brandy* book was a success. She allowed
herself to feel the emotions through the drawing, the writing.

And she knew all about being an orphan.

All about what that little boy would be feeling.

She was pretty sure she even knew what his big, rugged uncle was feeling under all that expressionless machismo.

Matt Donahue's eyes were not expressionless. Not at all. His eyes held pain and bewilderment and if the way he looked at his nephew was any indication, he had a huge capacity to love.

A capacity that had probably left him as wrung out as a cloth going through a ringer.

It just wasn't possible to be her nasty normal self under those circumstances. Not that she was really nasty, but she did such a good impression of it that most people were fooled.

Not her sisters, though.

They seemed to know who she really was, even when she was not always so certain of that herself.

The thing to do would be to get the blinking fence done so that she could be rid of him. Thank him for being a nice neighbor, and see him off, hopefully never to return with his little boy who looked so lost.

And with his own dark eyes fixed on her with such steadiness she thought uneasily he might be able to see her very soul.

A man's eyes being so deep and dark like that, so thoughtful and so tinged with sadness could make a person feel weak.

Could make a person hope that the same kind of miracles that happened to her sisters could happen to her.

She drained the pop, tossed the can, and tried to remember where she had put down her hammer in all this long grass. She searched for fifteen minutes feeling his eyes on her the whole time, his expression amused. She had the awful feeling he knew where that hammer was, precisely, but that she'd have to ask before he told her.

By the time she found it, her sympathy for him had waned completely. She resented the laughter in his eyes. She resented the ease with which he pounded a three-inch nail. She resented that her fences needed his attention, and that she had done it all wrong without him.

And she resented that her sisters had been given miracles, and had enough trust and love in their hearts to accept them when they happened.

She was far more cynical.

All her resentment seemed to build inside her, and she put it into her next hammer swing. She could feel the power in it. She was going to drive that nail right into next week. Best of all, she was going to show him that she could drive it into next week, show him that she didn't need him or anyone else, show him—

Somehow she missed the nail completely, and the full weight of that hammer, driven by fury and frustration, hit the base of her thumb. She heard the sickening crunch of the bone, and for a moment felt nothing.

For another moment, she actually kidded herself into believing she didn't even have to let him know. That she could bluff her way through this one.

But then the pain hit.

A sound escaped from her mouth, small and plaintive before she bit it back. Out of the corner of her eye, she saw him glance toward her. Holding her wrist with her other hand, she went down on her knees, cradled the hurt hand against her stomach, rocked away the pain.

He was beside her in a second, down in the grass with her, forcing her gently to give up her hand to him.

"What happened? Your hand? Let me look."

And then he was prying her hand away from wrist, unfolding her fingers, his face and voice so calm and soothing.

Dumbly she registered that his hand felt exactly as she had known it would when she had refused to shake it when he had introduced himself. Six days ago. Exactly.

His hand was firm and warm and leather-tough. Everything he was, was in the touch of that hand. His strength. His passion.

What she never would have guessed at was the tenderness, his power held in check as he looked gravely at her hand.

He looked into her face, and she noticed, absurdly that his lashes were way too thick for a man. And that just a trace of stubble darkened his cheeks. She noticed that he smelled of man smells. Horses and hay and leather and underneath all that, cleanliness. She could smell soap and shampoo.

Far away, in another compartment of her brain, panic was setting in. It was her right hand. Her drawing hand. She had a deadline. She had a cabin to clean. She had a donkey to look after.

His voice cut right through the panic, a voice she knew had tamed many frightened things. It was a voice that was deep and steady.

"I don't think your thumb is supposed to look like that," he noted, his tone deliberately no-big-deal. "Black-and-blue and bent funny."

"I'm okay," she said. "Leave me alone."

He looked at her sharply, masked his astonishment. His voice never altered. "We'll just go get Robbie from the barn. The donkey probably won't be happy to have story time interrupted, but I think a visit to the hospital might be in order."

"I'm not going to the hospital."

He raised an eyebrow. "Who said anything about you? Maybe I'm going to take the donkey to the hospital. Since you're incapacitated, I could have the evil deed done on him, and then we wouldn't have to give another thought to this fence."

Right. Add that to the deadline, cabin and donkey. A fence to build. She could not have a broken bone in her hand. She could not.

"I'm not incapacitated," she said, hoping by speaking the denial out loud it could make it true. But she was aware of forcing her voice out through thick layers of pain.

He looked very sober. "Thank goodness for me, it looks like your hitting hand is out of commission."

She gazed at the plum where her thumb used to be. "I can hit left, too," she said.

He laughed. He actually laughed, and it was the most reassuring sound in the world, a wonderful sound, a sound that she thought, even through the haze of her own pain, that he had not made for a long, long time.

He put his shoulder under her arm and lifted her to her feet as easily as if she was made of straw.

"Can you walk? Or do you want me to carry you?"

"It's my thumb, not my toe." *Don't carry me, don't carry me, don't carry me, God, as if I were a child again. Longing to be picked up, held, cherished.*

"Thank you for pointing that out to me. I have a tendency to get these minor points of anatomy mixed up." All the time he was talking, his drawl sliding across her skin like silk across the back of her neck, he was moving her toward her own barn.

Even though it wasn't her toe, the pain was making her sick to her stomach. She stopped for a minute and took a deep breath.

He took one look at her face and scooped her up in his

rms. She didn't even protest. For a moment she was rigid gainst him.

And then, pain-wracked, she let go just a little bit. She nuggled a little deeper into the broad plain of his chest, llowed herself to feel his warmth and strength.

Allowed herself to acknowledge that he was looking fter her, she was letting him, and it felt so good.

It was only then that she broke rule number one.

She started to cry.

Chapter Four

Robbie was no longer in the barn. Corrine had stopped sobbing but was pale, and nearly trembling in her fight for control. Matt knew she did not want to collapse entirely, that she was fighting with everything she had not to give in and soften against his chest.

He wanted to tell her it was all right, to let go, but somehow he knew it would take more than a suggestion from him to make this woman let go.

He had a very naughty thought about where he'd most like to see her let go. The thought was like being smacked up the side of the head. Where had it come from? Looks aside, she was too standoffish and too complicated to be attractive.

At least a sane man would have known that.

But then his hold on his sanity seemed to have slipped with the arrival of the damned donkey. Against his better judgment Matt Donahue had intertwined his life with hers—largely to impress his sister who was dead. Did it come much crazier than that?

Oh, yes it did, for his sanity had slipped a little more, working beside her, seeing her acting so fiercely and proudly independent when the truth was she could barely swing a hammer.

And now his sanity was being nudged right over the edge by this other contradiction: that she acted so damned prickly, and was so soft to hold, and that she acted so damned hard, and yet she fell to pieces like shattered glass over something so simple as being helped, and held by another human being.

Only it wasn't that simple. Her weight was sweet in his arms, and nothing had ever felt quite so complicated as holding her, his shirt wet with her tears, her warmth seeping into him, drugging him senseless.

"Robbie!" he called, impatient, and a little nervous. Now was not the time for his nephew to pull a disappearing act. Just when he was beginning to wonder if he had been hopelessly irresponsible in leaving the boy unattended, the front door to her little cabin burst open.

Robbie, to Matt's intense embarrassment, ran out the door of her house. Matt shot Corrine a look to see if she was offended, but she hardly seemed to have noticed.

Robbie was smiling widely until he saw her and then he skidded to a halt.

"What happened?" he whispered, terror leaping in his eyes.

Matt reassured him quickly.

"She hurt her thumb. That's all." Should he add she was not going to die? Carefully, casually, he added, "We're going to have to run her into the hospital. Hop in the truck. And for Pete's sake what were you doing in her house?"

"It's all right," she whispered. "I don't care."

"Well, I do," Matt snapped. "I don't want him wan-

dering into people's houses uninvited.'' Being in charge
of his nephew had made him uncomfortably aware of dan
gers he had lived with a blissful ignorance of up until thi
point.

"I had to go to the bathroom," Robbie said indignantly

Corrine laughed shakily. It was a rusty sound. A woma
who did not laugh enough. Matt told himself, firmly, h
didn't want to know why. And that he didn't want t
change it.

But another part of himself wasn't falling for it. He di
want to know why. He did want to change it.

Matt shifted her weight, opened the door of his truck
and slid her past the steering wheel into the center seat. I
put him, for a delicious and confusing moment, presse
hard against the softest parts of her, so close to her lips h
could see the soft grooves in them. He reared back s
quickly he smacked himself on the head, which was prob
ably exactly what he needed—a good smack on the head

Robbie got in the other side, and just as Matt started th
engine, out of the corner of his eye he saw Robbie lift up
so that his mouth was nearly in her ear, and say somethin
to her.

Over the roar of the diesel he had no idea what Robbi
said, but he felt her stiffen beside him. She swung he
head, and looked at Robbie with astonishment, and the
suddenly she relaxed, the rigidness leaving her, and she l
her shoulder touch Matt's on one side, and Robbie's o
the other. Robbie needed no further invitation to lean h
head on her shoulder, a look of blissful contentment o
his face.

She hesitated. With her uninjured hand she reached eve
so slowly, and ran the tips of her fingers through the feath
erlightness of Robbie's blond hair.

Some unguarded tenderness lit her face, and took Matt

breath away. She was not just pretty. She was beautiful, when that guarded look left her eyes.

She caught herself, yanked her hand away from Robbie's hair, and looked swiftly straight ahead. But she did not try to move her shoulder from underneath his head, nor, on the other side, did she try and move away from the pressure of Matt's shoulder.

He made it to town in seven minutes flat, which was a new record even for him, Miracle Harbor's most unrepentant speeder.

The hospital was located on a bench of land overlooking the town and the harbor, a view he'd seen a million times before, but which looked different today. Brighter. More in focus. He had the uneasy feeling the change in perception had way too much to do with that shoulder pressed against his.

The emergency department was empty and the duty nurse looked thrilled to have a customer. He found himself reluctant to relinquish Corrine.

"Could you call my sisters for me?" she asked, as the nurse led her away. "Abby and Brit." She rattled off two numbers.

He called the sisters, and heard her voice. Not her voice exactly, her voice with two very different regional accents.

But even though the voices had been so eerily similar to hers, nothing prepared him for the moment he glanced up from his magazine to see the outer door to emergency opening and Corrine walking in.

The same Corrine who had walked through the door to x-ray not half an hour ago.

No, wait. Not the same Corrine, because that Corrine had been wearing a shirt as yellow as dandelions and jeans faded nearly through, and this Corrine looked like she would have been at home on a Paris fashion runway.

To add to his confusion, yet *another* version of Corrine appeared, right on the heels of the Paris fashion plate.

Robbie, eyes wide as saucers, whispered loudly "There's three of her."

The women saw him and came toward him. Wrestling with his confusion, Matt unfolded himself from the uncomfortable vinyl chair.

"Are you Matt Donahue? Corrie's neighbor? The man who called? What happened?" The well-dressed one asked.

Not like Corrie at all, he thought gazing at the woman. Far more flamboyant, sure of herself. And the other sister had a kind of quiet serenity about her that Corrie didn' have either. How could three women look so alike, and their differences become so apparent in just seconds?

"We were, um, fixing her fences, and her hand got in the way of her hammer. I think her thumb is broken."

"Fixing her fences," the flamboyant one said, not showing much interest in the thumb. She sent her sister a look that spoke volumes, none of which he could interpret. Sh stuck out her hand. "I'm Brit and this is Abby."

He shook hands with both of them, and again noticed the differences between them, Brit's energy almost electrical, Abby's quiet and strong. He remembered Corrine not taking his hand at all when he had offered it to her that first day.

Less than a week ago, when his whole world had still been completely in his control.

Robbie, never one to be left out, came over and introduced himself, too.

Brit made the mistake of gushing over him. "Oh, he's so adorable."

When Robbie wrinkled his nose, Abby smiled at him.

"Ours is the best one," Robbie decided, folding his

arms over his chest and surveying the sisters analytically. Then he marched off to the toy bin and began to sort through it.

Matt felt a tide of heat burning up around his ears. Of course, her sisters wouldn't know Robbie was referring to Corrine when he said *ours*. As if he and his nephew had gone shopping and somehow ended up with the best triplet in the bin.

"Where is she?" Brit asked. "Is she all right?"

"She was in pain, but like I said it was her thumb. A long way from the heart." He could feel his ears getting hot again. "Uh, that's horse talk for not life threatening."

"Horses," Brit breathed. "You're a cowboy, then?"

"I raise quarter horse stock."

This earned the quiet sister a conspiratorial nudge in the ribs. Before she went for his life history, he said, "They took her through there. I'm sure she's waiting for you."

He just knew the sister called Brit would ignore that bright red No Admittance sign written on the door in two-foot-high letters.

Brit went over and gave the door a shove.

"I don't think you're supposed to go in there," he suggested, with absolutely no conviction. Triplet Brit made him very nervous. She had troublemaker written all over her. He noticed the rings sparkling on her fingers, and bet she was a handful for the poor guy she was married to.

"Oh, pooh," Brit said, with a toss of her head. "Are you coming, Abby?" Abby hesitated, gave him a wry grin and then followed her sister.

Good God, he thought, taking his seat. Three of them. It added to his sensation that his world felt like it had a funny tilt to it. Then it occurred to him, with her sisters here, he really had no cause to stay. But for some reason he stayed anyway, and it wasn't, if he was totally honest with himself, because of the fascinating articles in the March 1983 *Reader's Digest* he found in the waiting room

It was the gentlemanly thing to do, he told himsel sourly, make sure she was all right, not just dump her a the hospital and make tracks.

It seemed like a very long time later that her sisters came back out that door.

"She's almost done," Brit informed him cheerily, and then looked at him sweetly. "You don't mind running he home, do you? I've got an emergency at my business," she waggled her cell phone at him, as if she had just heard "and Abby has to get home to her baby."

Even without Abby's look of discomfort, he clued int the fact this might be a lie. He recognized exactly the species of troublemaker sister Brit was. A matchmaker But before he could slip out of the little noose being tosse around his neck, Robbie materialized at his side, took hi hand and looked solemnly at the sisters.

"Of course we'll take her home," he said importantly "She lives next door. She's *ours*."

Brit looked thrilled by that news, and Abby laughed Her laugh was beautiful, rich and full and melodious. made him wonder what Corrine's laugh would be like, she really let herself laugh. Brit hustled Abby out the door Matt suspected before she offered to drive her sister hom herself.

Moments later, Corrie emerged from behind the sam door. Her arm was in white plaster from her elbow to he thumb. Her eyes looked like they were going in two di ferent directions.

"Where are my sisters?" she asked, looking past hi at the empty room.

"They both had things to do. They asked me to tak you home."

She didn't miss the matchmaking angle either, because she turned bright red, ducked her head and took a deep breath, gathering herself.

When she looked back at him, there was no mistaking the "not-even-interested" set of her chin.

"That makes two of us," he muttered.

"Pardon?"

He wished her sisters, and Brit in particular, could have seen the look on her face. It was a look that iced any matchmaking efforts. In fact, had he been thinking of making a play, which he most definitely wasn't, Brit's help would have set him back several thousand yards from the goal post.

Which was a relief.

"I appreciate you taking me home," she said stiffly. He knew only good manners kept her from adding, *I would rather have gone home in the back part of a truck loaded with crocodiles, but my options seem limited.*

It was obvious to him she now intended to take back any ground she had lost in her vulnerable and pain-stricken state of a little while ago. She was not going to be the same woman who had sobbed against his shirt.

She managed to get Robbie in the middle on the way back, which Matt silently, seethingly told her was just fine with him. Who wanted her fragile little shoulder touching his?

He did.

He tried to ease the strain between them, get his mind rerouted from the fact it missed her shoulder pressed up against his. "You could have knocked me over with a feather when your sisters came in."

"That would have to be one heck of a feather," Robbie piped up.

She tried not to smile, and failed. It tickled her lips

before it disappeared. He hoped that meant she'd notice what a big, strong guy he was, undeserving of the title c auntie, not easily knocked down by feathers.

After a moment, he suspected she was trying not to ar swer, or struggling to strip the emotion from her answer

"That's exactly how I felt when I first saw them."

Here he thought he'd picked a safe neutral topic fc conversation, and even though she was trying so hard, sh could not disguise the pain in her voice.

"First saw them?" he echoed, puzzled.

"We weren't raised together. We were separated whe we were young."

That explained the different accents. He cast her a loo out of the corner of his eye. She was white with pair whether from the drugs wearing off, or from being raise away from her sisters he couldn't be sure. Don't ask, h ordered himself. Don't.

But there it was, his voice, defying orders from the big strong guy. "Why?"

"We don't know yet. We're trying to find out. There' this little old lady, Mrs. Pondergrove, who we're positiv is involved. But she's taken a sudden vacation, so w haven't been able to ask her our questions. Abby's hus band has a police background. He's been doing some dig ging for us. "

Leave it. A direct command. His voice again, complet mutiny. "And?"

She was looking at her cast with grave interest. "M parents were killed in a car accident when we were thre I went to live with my aunt, my mom's sister. For a whil I don't know why my sisters went elsewhere."

Her voice went all tight when she said *for a while*. H was going to file that for the time being. "So, when di you meet your sisters?"

"Just a few months ago. Here."

Her answer was clipped—a place she did not want to
go. He suspected there were more than a few places like
that for his lovely neighbor. And that those were the places
he needed to go the most.

But damned if he was taking her there. He was taking
her home. Period.

Well, fixing her fence, then period.

"I'm sorry." He couldn't think of anything else to say,
new from Marianne's death, there was nothing else he
could say.

She didn't say anything, and when he looked over she
was trying to awkwardly wipe another tear that was sliding
down her cheek.

"My mommy died, too," Robbie said quietly.

She said nothing, but out of the corner of his eye, Matt
saw her left arm, slip around Robbie's shoulders, and
squeeze. Her arm stayed there, too, for the whole six and
half minutes it took him to get her home. Driving way
too fast, and no emergency to blame it on.

Depending how you defined emergency. The riot of different feelings inside him, the mutiny of the voice box
troops, seemed like they might qualify.

"I like that there's three of you," Robbie decided, "and
I like that you're the best one."

She gave the little boy a look of such startled surprise,
Matt felt like his heart would break inside his chest. It was
right there in her face, bald and unvarnished. She had
never been the best one, ever. Not at anything, not in her
whole life.

There was a hurt inside this lady that was too big for
one man to handle. Especially a man like him who was
nursing a fairly major heartbreak of his own.

He wanted to drop her off and spin his tires getting ou
of her driveway.

But when he pulled up in front of her cabin, he jus
couldn't. How was she going to manage with her arr
slung up like that? The look on her face said she'd di
trying, but even if she could look after herself, the damne
donkey was probably more than she could manage.

Besides, his sister would frown on him dumping her of
and getting the hell away from her as fast as he could.

"You don't have to see me in," she said coolly.

"No, ma'am, I don't, but I'm going to anyway."

She looked like a hen with ruffled feathers. Robbie wa
already out of the truck and inside her house as if, on th
basis of one visit to her bathroom, he now was a co-owne
in the place.

The boxes that had been on her porch were now stacke
inside, but were largely unopened. He noticed a bedfram
and mattresses leaning against the wall outside the bed
room.

He felt something inside him slump.

"Have you got a place to sleep?" he heard himself ask
ing, his reluctance obvious even to him.

"The sofa will be fine. Thank you. I've been meanin
to unpack, but I've been spending a bit of time with th
donkey." At least she had the good sense to look sheepis
about that.

"My auntie will put together your bed for you," Robbi
announced, and came and took her hand and led her ove
to the couch. "You sit here. I'll bring you a soda. Aunti
has some in the truck."

Matt couldn't think of a graceful way to remind hi
nephew he did not want to be called Auntie in front of
gorgeous woman. Even one he was dying to get awa
from.

She looked like she wanted to refuse, but bit it back. ''Thank you,'' she said.

''Are you hungry?'' Robbie continued. ''I am. I could make you a peanut butter-and-jelly sandwich. Do you have peanut butter and jelly?''

''The one thing I've unpacked,'' she told him with a weak smile. ''My favorite.''

Well, there. She'd gone and won Robbie for life.

''I'll get the soda first.''

''That would be nice,'' she said, but Matt could tell every word cost her. Having this little boy care about her was stealing her pride, knocking down her walls.

He noticed he had been offered neither a soda nor a sandwich.

The door slapped shut behind his nephew.

''He's very thoughtful for someone so young, isn't he?'' she asked, leaning her head against the back of the sofa and staring at the ceiling.

''Unfortunately he knows more than a tyke should ever have to know about looking after sick people.''

''Oh, Matt.''

And just like that her walls were down, and he could see who she really was. And it wasn't someone tough and hard at all. It was someone so sensitive that she had built walls all around her so the world would never know.

Except he knew, now. It occurred to him this chink in her armor was far more devastating for him, it seemed, than for her.

''I'll put your bed together,'' he said gruffly, ''and then we'll get out of your hair.''

But of course life was never that simple. He put her bed together in about ten minutes, but then it looked so naked just sitting there, and he wondered how she was going to make it with one hand. So he gingerly started opening boxes in her bedroom until he found some sheets.

Not pretty sheets. Just clean and plain and white. The blankets weren't pretty, either. Gray wool, like something they might issue to someone in the army.

He felt bad that she didn't have pretty things and he didn't even know why. Maybe because when that wall had come down a few minutes ago, he'd glimpsed a woman who should have pretty things.

After he'd made the bed he came out, and found her and Robbie eating peanut butter-and-jelly sandwiches and sipping soda. Robbie invited him to join them, and he wanted to resist, but two separate parts of him wrestled, and the one that wanted to sit in her living room on boxes eating peanut butter-and-jelly sandwiches won. In embarrassingly short order.

It wasn't until he sat on an overturned apple box that he noticed the easel by the window, and the picture on it. A line drawing, very simple, of a girl's winsome face. Given the simplicity the amount of emotion the drawing captured was remarkable. He had a shadowy feeling of recognizing the face, but of course that wasn't possible.

He gobbled down his sandwich, while Robbie kept up a steady stream of potential names for the donkey. Fred. Harvey. Peanut head.

That made Corrie smile. "Peanut head?"

"Don't you think his head looks just like a big old peanut?" Robbie asked earnestly.

Matt certainly did think that.

"Buttercup," Robbie continued.

That made Matt laugh. "Perfect. That donkey's so delicate and lovely."

Robbie scowled, but Corrine laughed a little.

And just like earlier, it made Matt want to make her

laugh more. He tried out a series of ridiculous names in his head, but resisted the temptation to try them out on her, to see that laugh deepen until it chased the shadows from her eyes.

Instead he stood up. "You leave a mess in the kitchen?" he asked Robbie.

"No," Robbie lied with easy sincerity.

Matt went through to the kitchen and tackled the mess Robbie had made. He could hear Robbie's voice for a while and then it faded.

When he came out, the two of them were leaned together, shoulder to shoulder, fast asleep on her sofa.

He wondered at that. Robbie was slow to trust, especially after his mother's death. What was it about his prickly neighbor that his nephew found so irresistible?

Matt found he liked looking at her without her knowing it. It allowed him to study her far more frankly than when she was awake, glaring at him every time he slid a glance her way.

Sleeping, she looked as innocent as his nephew. Some wariness had fallen from her face and she was so beautiful she might have been an angel. Her bone structure and coloring were lovely, almost breathtakingly so when not combined with a hostile, wary look.

He sighed, went and picked up his nephew, nestled him into his shoulder, and glanced back at her. He sighed again, went and took the blanket off the freshly made bed, and tossed it over the sleeping woman.

He wished he could fool himself into thinking he was walking away for good.

But he knew he'd be back.

The excuse would be duty. Help her with the damned donkey. Maybe move a few heavy things for her.

The truth was more troublesome. He felt tugged to her

by some invisible cord, in some way he did not understand she was as irresistible to him as she was to his nephew.

Corrine awoke feeling groggy, her mouth dry and fuzzy as if her tongue had grown fur. She shifted, and moaned at the pain that shot from her thumb to her arm. She shot a resentful glance at the cast, only to see the cast was covered, as was the rest of her, in one of her blankets.

That bothered her. That she had fallen asleep with Matt in her house. It must be the drugs, because she didn't trust people that much, rarely allowed herself to be so vulnerable.

Though if she was going to trust someone, she grudgingly admitted, he wouldn't be the worst choice in the world.

She felt a ripple of awareness, followed by a blush that made her thankful she was alone, when she thought of him scooping her up yesterday, carrying her across her yard.

Would he think it was funny that she had never been that close to a man before? So close that the scent of him, strong and clean and mysterious, filled her every sense? So close that she could feel the iron bands of his muscled arms through the fabric of her jeans with such intoxicating intensity that her legs might have been bare? So close that she could feel the strong rise and fall of his chest, and hear the steady rhythm of his heart?

Matt Donahue oozed quiet strength. He was the kind of man people relied on—his old-fashioned sense of honor was evident before he even opened his mouth. It was in the way he stood, so proud and tall and sure. It was in the steady gaze of his eyes, and the firm line of his mouth. It was in the hands that had been hardened, and the shoulders that had been made broad by years of honest, physical work. It was in the way rugged features softened each and every time he looked at his nephew.

Not that she wanted to be thinking about his eyes or his mouth, or the set of those enormously wide shoulders while she was in such a terribly weakened state.

It had been a long time since she had thought in terms of trusting anyone but herself. Except her sisters. She had trusted them instantly.

A mistake, she now saw, since they had rushed to the hospital, only to send her home in the care of her neighbor.

"Devastatingly attractive," Brit had proclaimed him.

Of course, Corrine should have remembered she could not trust Brit in the man department. Her first gift from her sister had been that horrible book, *How To Find the Perfect Mate.*

And that was before Brit had sampled love's nectar herself. Now that she had found the perfect mate, Brit was incorrigible in her enthusiasm to see the whole world in general—and her one unmarried sister in particular—walking down the aisle.

"Mrs. Pondergrove is having another wedding dress made," she'd informed Corrine enigmatically, as if that was as good as a glimpse in a crystal ball.

"But you said she's away," Corrine had protested.

"She is. She sent the pattern to Abby from somewhere in Wyoming. Poor Jordan. He's having a fit not knowing where she is."

Jordan was Brit's new father-in-law. According to Brit, who was the triplets' undisputed and self-proclaimed expert on all things romantic, he was carrying a torch for Angela Pondergrove.

Corrine would have had to have been blind not to have seen the romantic hopes blazing away in Brit's eyes as she had grilled Corrine about the accident, but worked around to the breathtaking handsomeness of the neighbor as often as possible.

"And his little boy is adorable," she had breathed, and then looked momentarily panic-stricken. "Matt's not married, is he? He can't be!"

Corrine had glared at her while the doctor wound yards of wet plaster around her arm.

"Yes, he's married," she snapped, hoping that would be the end of it.

Brit was not that easily sent off trail. After regarding her sister for a full minute, she announced she was going to ask him.

Mortified at the thought of him *knowing* they were in here discussing his marital status, Corrine had given in.

"Okay, okay. He's not married. Robbie's his nephew. Robbie's mother died."

Abby seemed to understand the sadness of that event deserved a few moments of silence, but it held Brit in check only for a moment, before she blithely continued the interrogation about the neighbor's proximity, how they had met, the arrival of the donkey and the heaven-sent—according to Brit—gift of falling-down fences.

Corrine had smelled a matchmaking plot when Brit had looked at her watch, squeaked and announced she and Abby had an emergency to attend to, that Matt Donahue would have to drive Corrine home again.

Brit's acting was enthusiastic if not convincing.

But her desire to match Corrine with Matt only made Corrine's desire not to be matched with him greater.

Even if she could trust him.

If it had been a long time since she had trusted, it was an even longer time since she had allowed trust to be placed in her.

Like that little boy's.

She felt a funny squeezing in her chest, which she tried to blame on her sore thumb.

She closed her eyes and relived that moment just before they had driven to the hospital after the accident. Matt, so close to her as he leaned into the truck with her, so close to her that his chest was hard for a second against her breasts, so close that he could have brushed his lips against hers almost by accident.

Her senses still reeling from that close encounter of the loveliest and most terrifying kind, she became aware of Robbie, his lips to her ear.

"I've waited for you. I prayed for you to come."

She had been so astounded the pain had disappeared from her thumb.

How could he have waited for her? And prayed for her to come? And how on earth could she tell him whatever it was he had waited for and prayed for it certainly wasn't Corrine Parsons? How could she say in the face of his childlike faith that she was something she wasn't?

And then later, he had so resolutely chosen her above her sisters. *She's the best one.*

How could she live up to these things?

She did not want his trust, and yet could not deny the warmth that spread through her when she thought of it.

"What's happening to my world?" she demanded of the ceiling. "First a broken-down donkey, and now a little boy. I'm not going to love either of them, so don't even think it."

She felt immediately foolish. Who was she talking to? And who had asked her to love the boy or the donkey? Who would ask Corrine Parsons to love anything? Her heart was cold within her.

Funny, though, when she thought of the word love, it was not Robbie or the donkey that came to her mind.

And her heart did not feel quite as cold as it had before.

It was Matt Donahue's quiet brown eyes resting on her that she thought of, and that warmed some place within her that had been ice.

"The good kind of ice," she reminded herself impatiently, "the protective layer."

She threw back the blanket and got to her feet, staggered a bit from the effect of the drugs, went into her kitchen and rummaged one-armed and determined through her boxes. In time she found a can of beans, and after a horrible struggle that let her know just how helpless she truly was, she managed to open them.

She ate them cold.

Independence didn't taste nearly as good as she wanted it to.

Chapter Five

The phone rang, and Corrine picked it up. Had she been hoping it was *him?* How pathetic.

"Am I interrupting something?" Brit asked hopefully.

"Yes, a candlelight dinner for two," Corrine said.

"I'm thrilled. I'll hang up right away. What are you serving?"

"Canned beans for me. Carrots and hay for him."

"Oh, Corrine, I hoped Matt was there!"

"Well, he isn't, but the donkey is a fair replacement."

"Corrine, I hear something in your voice. Are you mad at me?"

"Yes."

"But why?"

"You sent me home with him. When I needed you."

"I just so want for him to be *the one.*"

"I don't believe in *the one.*"

"Well, neither did Abby, and look what happened to her!"

"I'm not like Abby. And I'm not like you. There isn't going to be a fairy-tale ending for me."

"There is if I have anything to do with it!"

"You won't!"

"Okay. Would you settle for some jelly doughnuts from my bakery and some company? Abby and I are going to come over and do your unpacking for you."

Corrine had made the mistake of confiding in her sisters that she was not unpacked. Now this was the lesson sisters were teaching her. She could be rude and crabby and un-cooperative, and they didn't give up on her.

It didn't even seem to faze them.

"I can do it myself," she said half-heartedly.

"Of course you can, dear," Brit said soothingly, "and you can ride a camel across the desert and wrestle alliga-tors, too. But that doesn't mean you have to. Besides, Abby's got your curtains ready."

That Abby had gotten the curtains ready so quickly amazed Corrine. No one had ever made that kind of effort for her before.

Besides the curtains, Abby brought her a plate covered in tinfoil, with roast beef and mashed potatoes and two different kinds of vegetables. "Beans out of a can," she clucked disapprovingly, when she saw the half-finished can on the table.

And Brit brought her take-out Chinese. "I couldn't bare to think of you sitting here amongst all these boxes eating beans. How depressing."

Her sister obviously had no idea what depressing was really like.

Still, Corrine thought a person could get rather accus-tomed to being cared about. Her sisters worked feverishly, and soon had an amazing amount done. The curtains were hung, bright yellow checked fabric that made the cabin so cheerful. There was a matching tablecloth, and a curtain to cover the doorway into her bedroom. Corrine stumbled along behind them and did her best to help, but mostly got in the way.

And her sisters never once told her she was a nuisance.

Or that she could have done it better.

Or to get out of the way.

Instead they fussed over her, and admired her few meager possessions, and oohed and aahed over her boxes of drawings. Finally, Brit made tea.

Corrine felt like she knew them, and had always known them and would always know them. Even after she left here, she would have these memories, of the three of them sprawled out on her furniture, sipping tea and laughing.

Well, they laughed and she smiled indulgently, basking in the reflection of their warmth.

"So, Abby, tell all about this new wedding dress," Brit said, pretending not to even care if Corrine was listening.

"Well, as you know, Angela Pondergrove gave me the dress I was working on for my wedding, and then she gave you the dress I was making for her after that. And now she's ordered a third one."

"It's for you, Corrie!" Brit crowed.

"I would never wear something like that," Corrine said with a shudder. "And I've decided I won't get married. Not as long as it's a condition of my inheriting this place."

"What?" Brit said.

"It's not like I was planning on getting married anyway. But I won't ever be coerced into it. Not ever."

"But I didn't feel coerced," Abby said.

"Me either," Brit said.

"Well, I would," she said firmly.

"Oh," Brit said glumly. "Is there any point in asking Abby what the new dress looks like then?"

"No," Corrine said.

"It's not exactly a dress," Abby said. "I mean it's gorgeous. But it's a pantsuit in white silk, with this beautiful flowing top, and wide-legged trousers."

"Would you wear a pantsuit?" Brit asked Corrine.

Corrine glared at her and didn't say anything. Brit, unoffended, threw a pillow at her.

"Aside from the pattern, I don't suppose anyone's heard from Angela?" Brit asked. "Mitch said his dad is going to die of a broken heart if he doesn't hear from her soon. Isn't that romantic? And at that age!"

"I hope everything's all right," Abby said worriedly. "She didn't say much of anything in the note she sent with the pattern. Shane's still working on tracking her down. He thinks she's gone to Minnesota. He said when he knows anything important, he'll let us know."

"I bet I could get it out of him—"

"And he said 'to tell Brit not to bother.'"

"Oh, bother," Brit said in a tone just like Winnie-the-Pooh. Abby laughed out loud, but Corrine didn't. Why would Angela be going to Minnesota? Corrine was the only one of the three sisters from there. Was Angela going to find out something about her?

After all those foster homes, there had been an incident with the law, too. Minor, it had been enough to scare Corrine into a different set of choices.

But how would her sisters feel if they knew about it? How would her neighbor feel?

When Brit looked at her watch and said she had to go, Corrine was sorry. She didn't want to be left with her thoughts. Abby lingered.

Finally, she too pulled on her jacket. "I hate to go," she said. "Corrie, I love being with you."

Corrine felt her lower lip tremble stupidly. Okay, so nobody had ever said anything like that to her before.

Abby came and put her arms around her and hugged tight. "You know what? I'm going to love you until you love yourself."

The next morning, sulking about her arm, Corrine found coffee, still hot, and a doughnut, in a box on her front step. She couldn't believe it had been left there without her noticing. The paper cup, labeled Heavenly Treats, told her the coffee was from Brit's bakery. It changed the whole tone of her day.

The next day, it was there again.

And the day after that.

She phoned Brit that night and told her to quit wasting gas. "All the way out here and all the way back into town, and you don't even stop to say hi?"

"I don't know what you're talking about," Brit said, genuinely surprised. "Coffee? And a doughnut? Maybe Abby."

But when Corrine called Abby she was not the coffee bandit, either.

Then Corrine knew who it was. And felt the breath leave her lungs. "Nice things don't happen to me," she said out loud.

"Can I ask you to do a little experiment? For me?" Abby asked.

The truth was if her sister asked her to jump off the roof with a homemade parachute she would have done it.

She listened.

"This is the experiment: just for one day I want you to believe good things can happen to you."

"That's silly," Corrine said.

"Maybe. But please, will you do it for me? It's only one day."

Corrine smiled reluctantly. "Okay. Just for you. Wha day?"

"Oh, tomorrow will do."

After she'd talked to her sister, her little cabin felt sud denly empty, even though the furniture was now arranged the boxes emptied and the curtains and pictures hung.

She awkwardly buckled a sweater around her shoulder and went into the crisp night air and out to the barn, hug ging herself.

Matt Donahue had left her the coffee and doughnuts Driven all the way to town every morning, for her.

The donkey raised his head when she came in, and looked hopeful. She realized his affection for her seemed to be connected with it being her hand passing him the hay, but she didn't mind.

"Hi," she said softly.

No reply.

Well, it wasn't as good as her sisters, but on the other hand she could tell him anything. Brit was another story.

"I could never wear one of those fluffy wedding dresses," she told him, then laughed nervously as if she had admitted something—that maybe, even without the dress, she did long for what her sisters had found. So what In a secret place inside of herself she harbored the same dreams as everyone else. No one had to know.

"Especially not Brittany," she told the donkey. "She'o go into overdrive. Revamp that awful ad she once wrote for herself to find *me* a husband."

The donkey stopped eating, and was eyeing her, chew ing complacently.

"Who needs a husband?" she asked. "I've already go an ass." She laughed nervously at her own humor. "You

ee, the way I grew up, I feel scared of some things. Re-
ationships. Commitment. Okay, maybe even men.''

The donkey made a noise.

''Present company excepted, of course. Because I didn't
row up in a regular family, I'm scared that I don't know
ow to have one. I've only learned how to look after my-
elf, not how to care about anything.''

It occurred to her that the donkey might be a not bad
eacher. She was learning to care for something. Who
ould have known that what Corrine Parsons needed,
ore than anything in the world, was to learn to care about
omething?

The donkey made his way idly over to where she stood
t the fence.

''If I ever did get married, though, I think I could go
or a pantsuit in white silk. What do you think?''

The donkey appeared to nod thoughtfully.

''You know with an eyebrow trim and a good brushing,
ou'd be a pretty handsome guy.''

His ears waggled.

She reached out her hand, and he pushed his furry fore-
ead up against it. For a moment she froze, and then very
arefully she scratched.

The donkey sighed with contentment.

She dropped her hand abruptly. God, what was she do-
ng? Out here talking to a donkey. It was quite pathetic, if
ne thought about it.

After making sure he had enough water, and doing a
ne-armed toss of an extra flake of hay, she scurried out
f the barn. She made a point of not saying good-night.

But he did. The strangest rusty little rumble came from
is throat.

Inside her snug little cabin, she contemplated the strange
nfolding of her life. Sisters. A mysterious donkey.

A beguiling waif next door.

And Matt Donahue.

And Abby's experiment.

*Just for one day…believe good things can happen t
you.*

Putting on her pajamas she felt a strange little thrill,
feeling like she had never ever felt before. She did nc
want to contemplate it, afraid it would dissipate like smok
under analysis.

But she felt oddly happy to be exactly where she wa
in her life.

She awoke in the morning to the sound of a hammer
She opened one eye, looked at her clock, and closed i
again. What was her obligation? To go visit him? Hel
him? She wanted to do both.

But she didn't want to look like she wanted to do tha
so she pulled the covers over her head.

Today was the day, she reminded herself, that goo
things could happen.

She became aware she was not alone. She was not eve
sure how she knew, but there was another presence in th
room.

She peeked under one corner of her blanket.

Robbie was waiting eagerly. "Good morning. Aunti
said I'm not to wake you up. I'm just to visit the donkey."

"Is there a donkey in my bedroom?" she asked, wid
ening her eyes and sneaking a look around the room.

Robbie chortled happily and came and leaped on th
bed.

"Auntie brought you some coffee and a doughnu
Should I get them?"

She had to close her eyes against pleasure so intense i
was almost pain. It was him. People cared about her. Ma
Donahue cared about her. *Her.*

Nobody had ever brought her things before, and now it seemed an endless stream of caring was pouring into her life.

Maybe luck changed.

Maybe good things *could* happen.

Just like that.

Maybe you used up your quota of bad luck for a lifetime, and all the rest of it was good, a little voice in her head suggested.

"Should I bring it?" he asked again.

"No. You go say good morning to the donkey, and I'll get dressed and bring my coffee outside to the barn."

"I took a small bite of your doughnut," Robbie confessed. "Just to taste. I had my own but it was a different kind. Don't tell Auntie, he'll say I'm not polite."

"Your secret is safe with me."

When the bedroom curtain closed behind her pint-size visitor, she went to her closet and threw open the door. What did she have besides jeans?

Nothing.

Well, the pantsuit that she'd worn to meet her editor once. Red and sleek, not at all what one wore to sip coffee in the barn with a donkey.

Still, she swiped the sleeveless tunic from it, and tucked it into her newest pair of jeans. After a long time in the bathroom, trying all kinds of things with her hair, she left it down.

It made her look very young, she thought.

And hopeful.

That's what was different this morning. A light shone in her eyes. Hope. She hoped that Abby knew what she was doing.

She went outside, and the light from the day seemed dazzling. Her coffee, still steaming, was in a plastic cup

with a lid on the porch. A chocolate long john with *tw*
small bites missing from it, sat beside it.

Long johns for breakfast.

She decided she could be the kind of girl who ate lon
johns instead of oatmeal for breakfast.

She came into the barn, and her eyes adjusted to th
light. Robbie was standing at the enclosure fence, his han
outstretched.

As she watched, the donkey slowly walked over to th
boy, lowered his head by that outstretched hand, and a
lowed Robbie to scratch his eyebrows, just as he had don
for her last night.

She didn't move until the moment passed.

The donkey wandered back to his hay, and Robbi
turned and looked at her, beaming.

"I tell him all my secrets," he announced.

She smiled. "Me, too."

"I didn't know grown-ups had secrets," Robbie said.

"A whole lifetime's worth."

"Lets go find Auntie."

"All right."

Matt was standing in the long grass, and had taken hi
shirt off in the early morning sun. He was a beautifull
made man, his muscles etched in the taut, hard surface c
his skin. The artist in her marveled at how he was com
posed: sun drenched, hair falling over his brow, muscle
rippling, copper-colored skin, faded jeans hanging fron
narrow hips.

The woman in her marveled at how she had spent
lifetime never feeling this.

The sudden stirring of interest. Of desire.

She felt suddenly faint with fear. As if she would tur
and run like a deer across the grass before he even knev
she had come.

But he chose that moment to turn, and glance over his shoulder. He straightened slowly, and looked at her.

Run, she told herself. *Run away and never look back.*

But another part held her firmly in check.

And yet another part whispered, *Take a chance. Give yourself to the day. Don't think. Don't analyze. Don't look at the past. Or the future. Just rest awhile in the glory of this moment. Take a chance.*

She moved a step forward, and then another one. Robbie burst past her and his uncle went down and scooped him up and swung him around, the morning sun dancing around them, Robbie's laughter hanging in the air.

He set Robbie down as she walked nearer. "Hey," Matt said, "I thought of a name for your donkey."

"What?"

"Donkey-o-tee."

She laughed. She did not know where it came from. Somewhere in her belly. A sound as dazzling as the day.

She moved into the circle of Matt and Robbie's love.

"Thanks for bringing me coffee and doughnuts the last few days."

He ducked his head. God, shy, all of a sudden? "No problem."

"So, have you got a job for me?"

"Don't know. Can you handle something really complicated?"

"I doubt it."

"You can hold the nails."

She rolled her eyes. And held the nails. And watched Robbie chase butterflies and do somersaults and race the wind up and down the pasture.

And watched Matt, pounding those nails with easy strength, moving with such unconscious ease and masculine grace. His skin began to shimmer with a fine sheen of sweat. She could smell him.

And he smelled of good things: earth and sunshine, soap and sweat.

How could she have gotten to be this age and not know? That the way a man smelled could drug a woman. The way his muscles moved, the shape of his wrists, the depth of his chest, the way the blades of his shoulders moved, the curve of his neck, these things could make a woman weak.

They could make her believe good things could happen.

"Tag, you're it," Robbie crowed, tapping her on the leg, and running off.

Matt turned and smiled at her, and that smile made it okay. To play. To be free. To let go.

She touched his shoulder.

The skin felt better than she could have imagined. It made her hand want to linger there.

"Tag," she said, shy now, too, "you're it."

And then she took off running, shrieking with laughter as he carefully undid the tool belt, put down the hammer, and then came after her.

She ran through the grass, laughing and feeling as if her lungs would explode. She caught up to Robbie. "Matt's it."

"Oh, no, he's way too fast!"

She glanced over her shoulder. Oh, God. The artist in her loved this. The man running through the tall grass, all his power in the springing of his legs, the pumping of his arms, his light shining in his face.

Matt tapped Robbie. "New rules," he called. "Anyone over four feet, one leg only."

"But I've already only got one arm," she protested.

Matt began to bounce along on one leg, still incredibly swift.

Robbie picked easier prey.

"Can't tag the one who got you," he told her.

"Do you Donahues just make up rules as you go along?" she asked, taking chase after Matt, as Robbie yelled encouragement.

She didn't have a hope. He teased her. He slowed down until she almost touched him and then he would sprint forward with an incredible burst of speed, or change direction with such lightning swiftness she nearly fell over trying to keep after him.

Then suddenly he stopped.

And she piled into his back. He turned around, and regarded her, folded his arms over his chest. "You got me," he said smoothly. "Now what are you going to do with me?"

It was an invitation. She knew it. His eyes were suddenly not laughing at all, but taking in her face, her lips, her hair.

Just for one day, she was going to believe good things could happen.

She did something she wouldn't have done yesterday.

Or ever before.

She stood up on her tiptoes and she kissed his cheek.

She saw the stunned look on his face, laughed at her own boldness, and ran. But not very far before he caught her, wrapped his arms around her waist to stop her forward momentum and spun her around.

"Can't tag the one who got you," she informed him.

"I have no intention of tagging you," he said. And he dropped his mouth over hers, and took her lips.

He tasted of strength and tenderness. It was a tiny kiss,

playful more than anything else, but she backed away from him wide-eyed.

"I hardly know you," she whispered.

"I know," he said. "We could change that."

"Hey," Robbie said coming through the grass, "this is no fun if I don't get to play."

"I don't know if we should," she said.

He smiled slightly. "I don't know either."

"I think I should go. In the house."

"I think you should come have lunch with Robbie and I."

"Walt's?" Robbie said hopefully, completely oblivious to the undercurrents.

She knew she couldn't do this. It was insane. It was asking for trouble.

It was believing good things could happen. Just for one day.

"Do they have hamburgers?" she asked.

"The best," Robbie told her, slipping his sweaty hand into hers.

"Hamburgers it is," she said and felt so happy and so scared at the same time she wondered if she was going to cry.

Now, he'd gone and done it, Matt thought. Kissed her. Given in to the urge that had been needling him since he first saw her this morning.

Something different about her.

Her hair. Down and easy. Making her look younger and more free.

It was when she'd laughed, really laughed at his donkey name, that he'd realized whatever was different went deeper.

Had he won her trust by bringing her coffee? Such a

small thing. Why did he have the feeling her life had not had very many small gifts in it?

Trying to make it appear as if he wasn't studying her too hard, he had done just that. And realized exactly what the change was.

The wall was down in her eyes. She didn't look scared or wary or hostile this morning. Was it the painkillers the hospital had given her for her thumb?

No. He didn't think so. Her eyes were clear and focused, and she was alert, her movements natural, not sluggish or choppy.

Had she done something to her lips to make him keep noticing them? He tried to figure out if she was wearing lipstick and decided that wasn't it.

He could tell she was looking at him, and he could tell that she liked looking at him. She had the advantage, because if he looked at her as much as he wanted to, they'd both need to be in slings.

When she'd touched his shoulder, and told him he was it, he knew better than her what they were playing.

And it wasn't tag, either.

They were playing with fire.

That fire that burned between a man and a woman, leapt up when you least wanted it to, sometimes with the person who seemed least likely.

Chasing after her, watching her move, like a dancer, so light and agile and strong, his breath had started coming harder than a little running could have accounted for.

But it was the light in her face that made his heart swell up within his chest. The light in her face, as if she'd never played tag before, no, never played before.

That's what was different today. She was lit from within, and even as the sun's heat intensified as the day went on, so did her light.

"We don't have to go out for lunch," she said, "I can cook."

"No," Robbie said vehemently. "Walt's. Corrie eats canned beans. I saw them on her table this morning."

She blushed as if he'd said she smoked funny things.

"Not always," she said defensively.

"I think we'll go to Walt's."

She gave him a punch on his arm, light and teasing. "Okay. Walt's it is. I love hamburgers."

"Me too," Robbie said.

In the truck, she sat beside Matt. Her shoulder touching his today.

"You know," she said, "I've never done that. Played tag."

He shot her a look. "Never?" He knew she needed to tell him why. And he knew he couldn't ask. She had to tell him on her own terms. When she was ready. If she was ever ready.

"No," she said, "Never."

But she didn't add anything else, and she looked distant.

He couldn't bear to see the light fading from her eyes.

"Are we ready to take a vote on donkey names yet?" he asked.

"We need a few more names before we vote," she said.

And so he and Robbie entertained her all the way to town with names for donkeys. But she didn't offer any.

And Matt suddenly realized that naming the donkey was about something else. Claiming something. Staying. Believing, maybe.

On impulse, he took her hand in his, and squeezed it, then let her go.

She looked at him, wide-eyed, as though he had read her mind.

Lunch was great. She packed away food like a man—

two Walt burgers and a chocolate milkshake. She laughed lots.

He didn't ever want to let her go, but he had his own place to look after. When he asked her if she wanted to come over, he knew he'd pressed a little too fast.

Her not coming was about something else, too. Maybe the very same things. Staying. Believing.

He finished the fence the next afternoon. He willed her to come out the whole time he was working, but she didn't. He caught glimpses of her, though, watching him from the window when she thought he wouldn't notice.

After he pounded the last nail, he dropped off his tool belt at the truck and went and hammered on her door.

She opened it.

The walls were back up in her eyes, but not as high as before. Just a little nudge would probably bring them back down. Is that what he wanted?

"I thought you might like to let him out," he said.

She wanted to refuse, he could tell. She wanted to pretend it didn't matter to her. And maybe that Matt Donahue didn't matter to her, either.

But in the end, she couldn't hide how much she wanted to be the one to let her donkey out. And something in her eyes told him he mattered to her more than she wanted him to.

Well, that was a big ditto. Because she mattered more than he wanted her to, as well.

A moment later, with great ceremony, with Robbie cheering lustily, she unlatched the outside door of her donkey's stall.

He shuffled warily out into the sunshine.

"Oh," she said, "look how happy he is."

Matt could hardly tear his eyes from her radiant look of pleasure, but he finally turned and regarded the freed donkey. He tried and failed to detect happiness in the donkey's shrewd look.

The donkey lifted his head and sniffed the air. And then he took off running.

"He's beautiful," she said.

Matt was not sure that he had ever seen an uglier sight than that long-eared beast pounding down the fence line.

He didn't like the way the donkey was acting. An animal in a new pasture was usually cautious. Checked the perimeters at a walk, with lots of stops to sniff the air and taste the grass.

That donkey was running as if he had a mission.

And sure enough, he didn't even pause when he came to that back fence.

His muscles coiled and he rocketed smoothly off the ground and cleared the fence as if it were two feet high instead of five.

"He should be in the Olympics," Robbie noted happily.

"My donkey!" Corrine wailed.

"My mares," Matt said grimly. Life was wrested out of control again. He had the oddest feeling he might just have to get used to the fact that life planned to throw him some curve balls. He slid Corrie a glance. And those were some curves. Did a man surrender or fight? He supposed it depended where he looked. If he looked at Corrie's eyes, surrender. If he looked at the disappearing hindquarters of that mule, fight. And with that last thought he spun on his heel and ran for his truck.

Chapter Six

Robbie was fast asleep on her couch. Corrine had covered him with a blanket, and she noticed that his thumb had found its way to his mouth—a fact that probably would have mortified the independent tyke in the light of day. As he slept, his lips closed tight around the thumb, he gave a powerful, contented pull on it.

It reminded her how small he was, how very young, how terribly vulnerable. And what a fragile thing was his trust in her. A trust that had been placed in her unquestioningly from the moment he had leaned toward her in the truck.

I've waited for you. I prayed for you to come.

She couldn't believe that anyone would pray for her to come to them, but then ever since Matt Donahue had become a part of her life, she felt different, as if she was changing in some fundamental way, perhaps becoming the kind of person someone might like to have in their lives.

If she didn't have a clue who she really was, how did a five-year-old boy?

And why did she think she could see who she really was in the enigmatic darkness of Matt's eyes?

She had not seen Matt again since her donkey had hopped the fence hours ago. It was now after ten. She assumed that meant her donkey was still on the loose.

The phone rang, and she hoped it was him, but it was Abby. She wondered, uncomfortably, what it meant that she was disappointed. Only a short while ago, hearing from her sister filled her with a spreading warmth that seemed beyond compare.

And the warmth was still there, but now she did compare, to a different kind of warmth. Entirely. The honest truth? She wished it was Matt. She wanted it to be him.

"Well, did you try the experiment?" Abby asked.

"I did," Corrine admitted.

"And?"

"The day was pretty nice." she said. An understatement. She thought back. Fixing the fence in the bright sunshine, playing tag, all squeezed together in the cab of his truck, eating those delicious hamburgers, discussing the merits of pickles.

It had been so wonderful it scared her. She had wanted to pull back, think about where she was going, not just drift there. She had to think about how vulnerable she was prepared to be, because it seemed to her Matt Donahue was going to expect more of her than she could give, want her to be more than she knew she was.

But even her effort to get things under control had gone awry. And now there was a little boy asleep on her couch.

It seemed so normal, somehow. Wholesome. A little peek at what other people's lives were like.

She thought of that kiss, Matt's lips brushing hers, playfully, yesterday afternoon. Well, maybe it would be

stretching it to call that wholesome, but still clean and
fresh. Invigorating. Excitement with no edge of danger to
it, unless emotions breaking free for the first time counted.

"So," Abby said, "you want to try it for one more
day?"

"Oh, I think my luck has taken a turn for the worse,"
Corrine said, as if she didn't care one way or the other.
She reported, "My donkey jumped the fence. Matt's been
out looking for him. If he finds him with his mares, I think
I'm in big trouble."

Abby said gently, "Corrine, sometimes even things that
seem bad are really good. If you believe good things will
happen."

Easy for her sister to be the eternal optimist. The home
she'd grown up in may not have been perfect, for what
home was, but at least it had been a home. It had been
evident at Abby's wedding her adoptive mother, Judy,
adored her.

Yes, Judy had wanted to control her, but only because
she wanted good things for her.

"Abby," she said, and she heard that stiff little note of
pride in her voice that she hadn't heard for a few days,
"it's a little late in life to convert me to a Pollyanna."

"Maybe I don't think so."

Well, what do you know? You haven't been there. But
she bit back the words, and even that told her she had
changed from the person she had been just a short while
ago.

When Abby started singing, *zippety-do-da, zippety-a,*
Corrine laughed. Even her laughter seemed easier, like it
had been locked inside her, and now that it had been let
out, fully intended to stay out.

"Promise me," Abby insisted, her voice suddenly quiet, intense. "One more day. What's one day?"

"Okay, okay. For one more day, then." She felt she was making the promise more for her sister than herself.

"Say it."

Corrine took a deep breath, "For one more day I'll believe good things can happen."

"To?" Abby must have heard the unspoken.

"Me," Corrine muttered.

"Good girl. I love you."

I love you.

Three tiny little words. Less than ten letters, total.

And yet they were words that could change the world. Her world. A world that had been so devoid of those words.

But at least she knew the value of those words, knew that they weren't to be bandied about carelessly, or passed off lightly. People seemed to say them all the time, as if they meant next to nothing. As if they had no understanding at all that those three words, *I love you,* were sacred.

After she hung up, she took the words in, sat on the edge of the couch with them burning inside her chest, at the end not inhabited by her small thumb-slurping guest, and contemplated them, reveled in them, and fell asleep.

She woke with a start when she heard the growl of the big diesel engine truck pull into the yard, and leapt up, feeling confused and disoriented and like an absolute mess. She smoothed her hair, retucked her shirt, wiped her sleeve across her mouth.

Matt tapped on the door, lightly, and even though she wanted to dash to the bathroom and brush her teeth and gargle and change clothes and have a complete makeover,

he stumbled to the door instead, threw the bolt and pulled
open.

She knew she was still partly asleep, because he was a
ream standing there against the black backdrop of a night
at had turned mean.

If he was annoyed that he had spent his evening chasing
er donkey, it didn't show.

He had on a faded jean jacket, the collar turned up
gainst the wind. The dark tendrils of his hair slipped out
om underneath a low-brimmed cowboy hat. His cheeks
ere whisker-roughened, ruddy from the weather.

"I woke you," he said softly, his voice suede and gravel
ixed. He reached up a gloved hand, as though he in-
nded to touch her cheek, and then let it drop before he
tually did. "Sorry, I didn't want you to think I'd for-
otten Robbie."

"I knew you hadn't forgotten Robbie. Why would you
ink such a thing?"

"You obviously haven't met Mrs. Beatle, you lucky
irl." He smiled, slow and unconsciously sensual, dimples
reasing the firm lines of his cheeks.

He was filthy. Lines of exhaustion ran around his mouth
nd under his eyes. His shoulders were slumped with wea-
ness. And he was still the sexiest man she had ever stood
is close to.

He smelled of horses and leather, and of the stormy
ight, and the mystery that was being a man.

"I would have called, but I didn't get near a phone."

She realized she was standing there gaping at him, and
e stood back from the door and let him in, trying not to
e obvious about how deeply she breathed in his scent
hen he moved by her.

"Any donkey?" she asked, wrestling the door closed

against the wind. She turned to him. In the fuller light, sh
noticed the smudge of dirt across his cheek, the rip in th
sleeve of his jacket. The band of his hat, and his coll
were dark with sweat.

"I got a rope on him once, but he dragged me about si
counties and then rammed me into a tree."

"Matt, I'm sorry."

He shrugged. "I'm going to grab some grub from hom
and then I'll head out again. I wanted to make sure you'
be okay with Robbie here for a while longer. Since I can
find the donkey, I'll have to move my mares."

"Tonight? In the dark? It looks like it's going t
storm." She glanced at the clock, and was amazed to se
it was close to midnight.

"Some of them are in heat. It's got to be done."

He said this with surprise, as if he couldn't believe sh
didn't know that it didn't matter if it was dark, and lat
or that the wind was howling, rattling the windows of he
small cabin.

And she knew this was who he was. His whole histor
would be about strong, rugged men, men who simply an
without complaint did what had to be done, no matter
it was dark or hard or cold or uncomfortable. He was
breed of man who pitted his raw strength against his ci
cumstances. It would never cross his mind to back dow
give up, admit defeat.

Men like him could be counted on. To do what neede
to be done. Every single time.

"They say you have to be careful what you name a
animal," he told her, a little spark of laughter runnin
through tired eyes.

"In what way?"

"Well, for instance, you don't want to name a hors

ronco, or Buck, because he'll generally live up to his
ame.''

"But my donkey doesn't have a name.''

"That's good, because I sure as hell don't want him to
ve up to Don Quixote.''

For a second she was baffled. Then she laughed. "I
ink you mean Don Juan,'' she said, and giggled. Actually
ggled like a seventh-grade girl in braces and her first bra.

He smiled back, not at all put out by his error. "I think
ou're right.''

She hadn't been around very many men with that brand
f strength, either. The kind with such an ingrained sense
f their own worth, that they had no problem admitting
rror.

"So, unless you have windmills, you should be okay.
ome sit at the table. I can probably rustle up some grub.''

sounded hopelessly corny. Not the type of thing Corrine
arsons said at all. Ever.

But then Corrine Parsons had never believed good
ings could happen to her before either.

"Don't go too western on me. I can't eat canned beans.
ot if my life depended on it.'' Another glimmer of that
nile. The one that made her heart leap in her chest, do
omersaults, jump up and down like a pom-pom girl.

Dimples should be declared illegal on men. Or at least
n ones who looked like him.

He shrugged off his jacket, glanced around and hung it
n a peg behind her door. He took off his hat and hung it
n the back of the door, too. It was like he was coming
ome, and her heart did a few more flips at the very
ought.

Praying the back flips of her heart were not evident she

said, "I can make other things. How about grilled chees
and soup?"

"Perfect." He moved by her, gazed at Robbie for
moment, the lines of his face softening. Then he turne
back to her. "Do you mind if I get cleaned up?"

"Through there."

In a moment, she heard the water running in her bath
room. And him humming, and thumping and swishing.

Man sounds.

Good man sounds.

How could the sound of him washing his face appeal t
her? In her loneliness, in her status as a single woman
somehow she had become pathetic. That was the only ex
planation.

Still, if she closed her eyes, she could picture him. Sh
bet he had his shirt off, and was leaning over her sin
sluicing water over his arms, his face, the back of his neck

When he came out of her bathroom it looked like h
had stuck his whole head under the tap. His hair was dam
and curling, little drops of water washed down his nec
into his shirt. He must have taken his shirt off because
was undone an extra button, as if he had pulled it back or
too weary to even notice that it was not done up all th
way.

Her eyes traveled down the column of his throat, to tha
enticing vee, and to the dark, springy hair that curled there
She had a sudden desire to go to him, and boldly slip he
hand through his shirt. Touch that hair, his skin, th
smooth, hard mounds of his pectoral muscles. She gulpec
and blushed, shocked at the direction of her thoughts.

And just a little bit thrilled by them, too.

He watched her, watching him, his gaze slow and lazy
And knowing. Not in the least shy or embarrassed.

She looked away first, feeling self-conscious and silly. He was obviously a man accustomed to being admired. She whirled away from him and began busily banging pots and opening cans. The food was going to taste like dust, he was so distracted.

The simple task of opening a can, with his eyes on her, suddenly seemed more difficult than running a marathon.

A tingling awareness turned her limbs to sand. A forbidden longing leapt into her with such power it made it difficult to butter bread without awkwardness. Her longing was not just to hold him, to touch him, to feel his lips again on hers, though certainly that was a delicious part of it.

But there was a deeper part, hidden, denied. And that part had little to do with the physical pull he exerted over her. She nurtured a newborn and secret longing that this could be her life. Ordinary. A man coming in from the cold every night, hanging his coat behind the door, sticking his head under the tap, and looking at her, long, and hard and lazy.

And if there could be something of the sacred in his eyes, that was all she would ever ask for.

She felt like a little girl writing her list to Santa.

And please, please, please, if I can just have this one thing, I will never ask for anything else ever again.

But that's what she needed to remember.

Her letters to Santa had never been answered. She was the girl least likely to ever have a dream come true, or a wish answered.

Except, she reminded herself wistfully, that's not what Abby thought.

And Abby had made her promise one more day.

"Penny for your thoughts," he said.

"I was thinking of Santa Claus," she responded, then wished she hadn't. Good grief. Santa Claus. She flipped the sandwich. Burned. Her nose so attuned to the pure soap-enhanced man fragrance in the room, that she had missed that little hint that his dinner was going up in smoke.

Maybe she needed to tell Abby it was far easier to make conversation when you could rely on sarcasm.

"Really?" he seemed fascinated. "Isn't it a little early to be making your Christmas list?"

"That depends what you're asking for." She slapped the sandwich on a plate, and gestured for him to sit down. The soup boiled over.

"What are you asking for?"

"The safe return of my donkey, of course." She knew she should make him another sandwich, but she couldn't. She'd probably burn the cabin down if she didn't get away from the stove. She sank into the chair opposite him, rearranged the wildflowers at the center of the table, tried to pretend looking at him didn't even remotely interest her.

"All I want for Christmas is my Donkey-O-Tee," he sang to himself as he munched his sandwich. His voice was deep, masculine, beautiful. Threads of lightness ran through it. "You're onto something with this Christmas stuff," he said and sang again, unselfconsciously "Doesn't that have a ring to it?"

She truly wished he wouldn't have said that.

Because that was the secret she was keeping, even from herself. She wanted it. She wanted rings and white dresses and picket fences and babies. She wanted what every girl in the world wanted.

A man to love her.

All those things that had come true for her sisters, and

n amazingly short order, too. They had both told her she
ould expect miracles, here in Miracle Harbor.

The thing was she hadn't believed them.

The thing was she was scared to death to believe them.

But maybe it would be okay to believe. Just for one
more day.

Matt had liked it when she had opened the door and
ooked at him, hair tousled, shirt wrinkled, eyes still a little
uzzy from sleep. He was no expert, but he was willing to
et it was a rare thing for a woman to look that damned
ood when woken in the middle of the night.

He knew what he *should* feel. Furious that her donkey
ad him riding fence lines on a dark night when the wind
ad come up off the ocean and felt like it could slice the
meat from his bones.

But coming out of a cold night into sudden warmth like
his was like drinking hot buttered rum. The heat began in
is belly, moved, slowly, languorously through him.

Was it the warmth of her cottage that made him feel
uddenly so mellow? Oddly content?

Or maybe it was the clean yellow towels in her bath-
oom that smelled of heaven when he pressed them into
is face. The jar of wildflowers on her table. The cheerful
urtains that matched the tablecloth.

Woman things, that a man didn't know he was missing
until he came face-to-face with them, felt them offering a
ilent sanctuary on a bitter night.

Or maybe it had been the look on her face when he
ame out of that bathroom. Really, blushing should be de-
lared illegal in women. Or at least in ones who looked
ike her.

It sure wasn't her grilled sandwich that had filled him

with this feeling of rare warmth, the kind of warmth a man
felt when the day's work was done, and the fire was lit
and a woman came to him, the promise of a different kind
of fire in her eyes.

Nope, scorched bread, and cheese not melted couldn't
be doing that.

Somehow the imperfection of the sandwich was endearing. She'd made it for him, bravely, one arm still out
of commission.

For him. A long, long time since anyone had done anything for him. So long ago, his memory didn't seem to
stretch that far.

It seemed to him, he and Corrine had covered a great
deal of distance in a very short time. The two people least
likely to do that.

Both too wounded, too battered by the storms of life.

Still, there it was. The look in her eyes and the warmth
in his belly, that had nothing to do with soup out of a can
as scorched tasting as the sandwich.

If he stayed here, he was going to kiss her.

He was in a weakened state. Tired. Cold. Still hungry.
She didn't know a thing about feeding a man. He could
have packed away about a dozen of those flimsy sandwiches, scorched or not. And he needed coffee, strong and
black, not this tea that smelled like it was made from the
same wildflowers that graced her table. For some reason
that small giveaway—that she didn't have a clue how to
look after a hungry, tired man, pleased him.

And didn't please him at the very same time.

It meant kissing her again could be serious business.

A whole lot more than a soft place to lay down an aching body. He allowed himself, briefly, to contemplate taking her wrist when she moved by him to turn off the whis-

tling kettle on the stove, tugging her onto his lap, putting his hand behind her neck, and bringing her lips down to meet his.

It was the kind of torment he could do without, considering the night he had ahead of him. He got up from the table so fast he knocked it over. He told himself it was because he couldn't drink any more of that tea, but he knew he was lying.

The empty plate clattered to the floor, and the wildflowers scattered. The jar broke in half and water joined his half-drunk tea in a pool on her floor.

He swore, and was immediately sorry and said so. Something in her eyes told him she had heard a little too much rough talk in her time.

And then they were both down on their hands and knees, picking up glass and stray flowers, and getting their knees wet, and suddenly they nearly knocked heads.

She sat back on her heels, and so did he.

He stared at her. The wild tangle of her hair, and the eyes that looked suddenly midnight blue, cheeks flushed, biting down hard on her bottom lip as if to keep it from quivering.

With desire.

For him.

Wildfire flashed through him.

It was going to happen anyway, that moment he'd hopped up from the table specifically to avoid.

It was just one of those things: destined.

Hadn't he known that from the very start? That there were elements of destiny in her coming here? Becoming his neighbor? Breaking her thumb?

Hadn't he known, from that small, almost playful meeting of their lips earlier, that it would never be enough?

That he would be tormented until he gave in, and tasted her lips again? That his waking thoughts and his dreams would be equally haunted by her?

She was leaning toward him, her beautiful curves pressed hard into her shirt, her chest rising and falling, her eyes half-closed with longing.

For him.

Flash-fire.

He leaned toward her, nearly touched, nearly—

"Who broke something?"

They snapped apart as though their heads were on elastic bands.

She scrambled to her feet and wiped her hands on her jeans. She was blushing again, her cheeks blazing, his own heat being reflected back to him.

"I did," Matt said getting slowly to his feet, watching her, commanding her to look at him. Telepathy—not a strength of his, apparently.

Because she looked everywhere but at him. She looked at Robbie, who was standing sleepily in the doorway, and then at her feet and her fingernails. She finally settled for studying the mess on the floor.

It reminded Matt, painfully, what it would mean to kiss her. Way, way too much.

"Did you find my donkey?" Robbie asked.

My donkey. Geez. It should have been enough to douse the fires, but it wasn't.

"Not yet. I'm just heading back out. Don't come in here. You'll cut your feet." *Go back to sleep. Can't you see you've interrupted something?*

"Can I stay here tonight? I like it here."

So, Robbie could feel it, too. Those little touches. The clean towels and the flowers. Marianne had been so good at things like that. Robbie probably missed them more than his uncle, who hadn't ever had them.

Or at least not since he'd moved away from home.

Once, it seemed a lifetime ago, he'd been engaged to a woman. A society girl from Portland. She'd had enough taste and sophistication for both of them. She'd liked flowers, too; her apartment always had white roses floating artfully in blown-glass bowls. And the bathroom had pure white towels, thick as pelts, that had always driven him to wipe his hands on his jeans instead. Her apartment looked like places you saw in the magazines that boredom forced you to look at in doctors' offices. He'd spent so much time in doctors' offices he actually came to understand his wife-to-be was emulating Martha Stewart.

His so-called fiancée had left him without a backward glance when Marianne got sick and it became apparent this was not going to be one of those quick and romantic deaths, like in *Love Story*.

How either of them had ever thought she'd be a rancher's wife now seemed to him the epitome of romantic absurdity.

She'd looked classy and had not an ounce of real class.

Real class—strength, and staying power and a toughness of spirit.

All things he knew, without a doubt, that Corrine possessed. Even though she was probably not even remotely aware she possessed them.

It occurred to him that Martha Stewart approved decor hadn't appealed to him nearly as much as those wildflowers in a jar, plain yellow towels, rough wooden floors.

"I'll look after it," she said of the mess. "You go." Was she as aware as he was that they were one millisecond from the danger zone?

"All right. Thanks. Thanks for—" he didn't want to hurt her feelings by saying snack, so he said, "supper." He went over and scooped up Robbie, hugged him hard and close, then put him back under the blanket on her couch. "I'll come for you in the morning."

"Could you bring me a doughnut for breakfast?" Robbie asked.

"Oh, I can make breakfast," Corrine said.

Matt was well aware doughnuts were not the breakfast of champions. But he was scared to see what Corrine Parsons could do to a perfectly innocent egg.

"I'll look after breakfast," he said, tucked Robbie in, kissed the softness of his cheek, touched his hair.

The boy could make a man believe in miracles, without even trying.

But he did not want to be this close to Corrine contemplating miracles. He followed her lead, focused intently on shoving the copper buttons of his jean jacket through holes that suddenly seemed too small. He refused to look at her again, but it didn't matter.

The soft puffiness of her lower lip was now burned into the fabric of his brain. He could see it, without looking.

But he couldn't taste it without tasting.

Fighting an urge to go and sweep her into his arms, and do what he damn well knew they both wanted to do, he left the bottom two buttons undone, rammed his hat back on his head.

It was a measure of the heat he was holding inside that the coolness of the wind felt good now, instead of biting.

He drove home, saddled a fresh horse, swung into the saddle, and rode into the inky darkness of the night. Riding a horse in these conditions, herding his mares and their new foals up to the paddocks by the barn took a single-mindedness of focus that he was unbelievably grateful for.

He would have slept easier if his fences were higher, but there wasn't anything he could do about that. He'd have to sleep with one ear open, listening for the sounds of a commotion. He was used to sleeping like that, listening for a mare having trouble foaling.

Satisfied he had done all he could do, he brought his saddle horse to the barn. The top half of his barn door had blown open and was banging against the wall. In his weariness, he must have forgotten to close the hasp.

He opened the lower part of the door, walked his horse through and flipped on the light. There were two open stalls, designed for tacking right inside the door, and he led his horse into the nearest one, slipped off her bridle and exchanged it for a halter.

At the other end of the barn he could hear Cupie Doll, moving quietly.

His fingers were cold, uncooperative as he loosened his latigo leather. Another noise from the other end of the barn. A noise that seemed out of place.

He stopped, listened.

Nothing.

He swung the saddle off the horse, settled it on his hip, slid the blankets off with his other hand. In the tack room, he exchanged the tack for a pail of brushes.

And froze again, not breathing, not making a sound.

That was not Cupie Doll moaning and grunting like that. Not unless she was contemplating dying. He dropped the bucket with a clatter, and raced down the walkway to the darkened stall at the back of his barn.

He stared in disbelief.

Cupie Doll stood placidly in her stall, munching contentedly. And tucked in behind her, he could see a long gray ear. And then another.

The donkey peeked warily over her back at him.

Matt took a step back, not believing what he was seeing. To get in here, the donkey would have had to open the half door of the barn, then jump the lower part of it.

Even while Matt's mind told him it was impossible for that donkey to leap four and a half feet from practically standing still to get in there with her, there was no denying it.

Impossible or not, the donkey was in there.

And the mare seemed damned happy about it.

An hour later he had separated them. It had not been an easy task, both the donkey and the mare intent on not cooperating. The donkey was now locked in a stud stall that had iron bars to the ceiling. It looked like a jail, and Matt hoped it acted like one, too.

He finally dragged his weary body to bed.

And listened to the sound of them calling each other plaintively all night, the donkey's bray like fingernails on a blackboard amplified, the mare sounding shrill and desperate, infuriated that a mere man thought it was his business to thwart nature.

He didn't want to contemplate what that meant in terms of Corrine Parsons.

Because the pull between him and her was getting mighty strong, too.

Maybe a man was kidding himself when he thought he could control certain forces. It would be like ordering the waves to stop crashing on the shore, the tide to cease its ebb and flow.

Tired thoughts, he told himself with irritation.

Of course he was in control of what happened between him and his neighbor.

One hundred percent, totally.

He thought of her lips and the night suddenly seemed way too long. The donkey seemed to be singing his song. Need, longing, desperation, natural urges, lust. The donkey's night-shattering cries held all those things.

As did Cupie Doll's whimpered responses.

"Matt Donahue, you've lost your flippin' mind," he told himself. He pulled the pillow over his head, and ordered himself to sleep.

And became aware he wasn't nearly as much in control as he wanted to be, or thought he should be. Because sleep refused to come.

Chapter Seven

Corrine woke to the most amazing feeling. A feeling of lightness that approached buoyancy. It was as if the sunshine that streamed in her bedroom window, brilliant, was also inside her, illuminating her soul. She glanced at her clock. Six-thirty in the morning.

And not a single urge to moan, pull the covers over her head, and go back to sleep. Instead she felt an eagerness, almost an urgency to greet the day.

She tumbled from bed, and walked on tiptoe to Robbie, who snored softly still on her couch. The blanket was on the floor beside him, and she picked it up and tucked it back under his chin.

Then she went and opened her door, and stepped out.

The boards of the porch were rough and cool under her bare feet. The bird song was riotous. The sun played in dewdrops and they shot out sparks of fiery blue and green and yellow.

She took a deep breath, and hugged herself.

"Today," she said, out loud, throwing her arms wide, "I believe only good things can happen. To who? To me!"

She laughed, realized her feet were cold, and went back in and stuck them in her running shoes. Feeling like all she needed to look like an Ozarks grandma was a corncob pipe, she sat down on her top stair. And breathed.

Air that smelled storm-washed and clean, faintly of the sea, and faintly of wetness.

She heard the diesel, debated jumping up and making a desperate effort to make herself look good, and found herself unable to do so. She was who she was. She watched as the truck came down the drive, her heart like a bird, fluttering, singing songs of glory in her throat.

A different Corrine would have remembered, with horror, that she was in her nightdress, and that it was not the least sexy.

It reached to her ankles, was high at the neck, and gathered at the sleeves. The flannel dotted with little yellow buttercups. No lace anywhere to be seen. Designed by someone who believed sins of the flesh were to be avoided, apparently.

Why had she bought it?

The truth? To keep her warm. It had never occurred to her that anyone, beyond the paper boy, was going to see it.

She touched her hair, confirming it was in a wild tangle.

And she didn't have on any underwear, and that was probably about as indecent as she had ever been in her twenty-seven years.

And she didn't care.

Didn't give a damn.

The new Corrine planned to be wild and free, on fire

with the life that leapt inside of her, that told her to take chances, and hope and believe.

She noticed, once she quit trying to capture a glimpse of him through the sun-glinting windshield, he had a horse trailer behind the truck.

Sure enough, the donkey brayed and stamped, just as Matt pulled the rig to a halt at the bottom of her stairs. She did stand then, to see him better when he came out of the truck.

He hopped out of the truck, his movements so fluid and masculine. He glanced her way. Froze when he saw her.

She drank in the sight of him, liking how the morning light put a soft edge on his hard lines, danced golden around him. He was in a different shirt this morning, dusty blue denim, white hat, form-hugging dark jeans. And if ever there had been a form made to be hugged it was his. Clean, long lines, a purity of composition that took her artist's breath away. And made her woman's breath come sharp and ragged on a gasp of pure appreciation.

"I brought your donkey," he said, finally, after the silence had lengthened unbearably between them, as if words might divert what was in the air between them, crackling and sizzling and threatening to explode out of control.

"I see."

The words did nothing, if anything the sound of his voice, tenderness and roughness combined, took her one step closer to the edge.

Or at least one step down off her porch.

He backed away from her, as if he was having trouble taking his eyes off of her, too. Finally, he tipped his hat over his eyes, turned abruptly on his heel, and went to the back of his trailer.

She followed him, watched the lazy jump of his arm muscle as he gave the back latch a mighty shove that released it from its cradle, before he lifted it.

"Was he hard to get in there?" she asked, peeking by him at the hindquarters of her donkey. The donkey looked like he was snoozing, his ears flopped over, his weight lifted off a cocked back leg.

"Uh, no."

"That awful man who delivered him said it took him hours."

"Yeah, well." He tugged on the donkey's tail, put a protective arm up to block her from getting in the donkey's path.

The donkey backed out of the trailer, slowly, calmly, and then stood regarding them both. After a second he yawned and gave his head a shake.

Corrine frowned. "That's not my donkey."

"How many donkeys do you think were on the loose last night?"

"He just looks, um, different."

"Yeah, well."

"And he's acting different, too." She put out her hand gingerly, and touched the donkey's shoulder. He groaned with pleasure and rocked back and forth against her hand, scratching his shoulder.

"Yeah, well."

"Why do you keep saying that?" She smiled at the way the donkey's velvety pelt felt under her finger tips.

"Because there's no delicate way of telling you what improved your donkey's temperament so damned much."

Her hand froze. She glanced up at Matt's face. She bit her lip. Oh, God. He'd probably kill her if she laughed. He'd kill himself if she blushed.

She could feel it. A tide of red coming right up her neck. Lucky that prim collar was so high.

"You *should* be embarrassed," he told her, not fooled. "Your donkey is disgusting."

"I'll take him to the barn," she volunteered, taking the lead rope and turning her back on Matt before he saw the shade of pink on her face deepening. Or before he noticed she wasn't properly aghast at her disgusting donkey. "I won't have any trouble with him, will I?"

Matt snorted. "Oh, no, he's just Mister Docile this morning. Worn out." It was his turn to blush, she noticed when she snuck a peek.

It was endearing.

"From braying all night long, in protest of his lock-up," he said hastily.

"Do you think—"

"Oh, he did the evil deed. It's just a matter of time before I know how much damage he did."

"I'm sorry."

"For a girl who is sorry, you're mighty close to laughing."

A chortle escaped. "That doesn't mean I'm not sorry."

A reluctant smile teased the sensuous curve of his mouth.

"Oh, go put your damned donkey away. I'll make breakfast."

The old Corrine would have had something to say about that. Would have never allowed things to go this far—for this easiness to exist between them.

This easiness overlaid with something else.

He narrowed his eyes at her, lowered the brim of his hat. "And Ms. Parsons?"

"Yes, Mr. Donahue?" she asked sweetly.

''When the sun pours through that nightgown like that, makes a man very receptive to apologies.''

She gasped, tried to hide behind the donkey, and when at didn't work, she picked up a clod of dirt and hurled at him.

He backed away, laughing, then turned on his heel, abbed a bag from the back of his truck, and whistling, aded up the stairs to her house, stepping over the broken e without even looking down.

Her face feeling like it was on fire, she led the donkey the barn, and returned him to his stall. The darkness ave the heat on her face a little respite, and she stayed in ere until she was pretty sure her color was approaching ormal.

She went back in the cabin door quietly, hoping to sneak hind him as his back was turned to the stove, but he oked over his shoulder and winked at her.

She darted by him and into her bedroom. As she closed e bedroom curtain, she heard his hoot of laughter. The rtain suddenly seemed like the thinnest of barriers be-veen them. He would be able to hear her getting dressed. 'ould he imagine it?

She had to wait for the flame to die in her face again, efore she emerged, her hair pulled back primly, her ouse done up to the highest button, not a sign of that anton woman who ran around outside in a see-through ghtgown.

Her house smelled heavenly. Not like a house at all. ike a home. She loved the smell of cooking bacon, and offee.

''Didn't you like my cooking?'' she asked. She was ring to pretend he didn't even interest her, but his back as to her anyway. So why not look? He had. She decided

she particularly liked the broadness of his shoulders, an
the narrowness of his waist where his shirt tucked into h
jeans.

"The honest answer, and the short one. No."

"It wasn't that bad."

"I didn't notice you eating any."

"That's only because I wasn't hungry."

"Your cooking explains why you're skinny as a ra
fence."

Skinny as a rail fence. Not flattering at all, but the loo
in his eyes when he glanced over his shoulder at her si:
zled more than the bacon in the pan. And suddenly, sh
was incapable of making small talk.

"Matt," she said softly, and took a deep breath, "you'r
going to kiss me today, aren't you?"

He turned again, and regarded her for a long momen
and then turned back. He tapped an egg and with one han
spilled it into the hot skillet. She should have let him coo
his own sandwich.

"Well, yes, ma'am," he finally said. "I guess I am."

"Could we get it over with right now?" she whispere

"Get it over with? You have the wrong attitude er
tirely."

"I know, but I feel like I'm glass about to shatter I'
so tense."

He didn't turn and look at her, but she could hear th
frown in his voice. "Nobody kissed you before?"

"Not the way you're going to."

He did turn and look at her then, and for a moment sh
stiffened thinking she saw pity in the intensity of his gaz
But when he smiled, she saw the softness in it and realize
it was gentleness.

"Not right now," he said.

She felt like she wanted to run out of the house and go own herself in her donkey's trough.

"You see, these things should never be rushed. There would be some hand-holding and eye-gazing that happens rst."

"Oh," she said.

"And there shouldn't be anyone under four feet high anging around taking notes and making comments."

"Oh," she said.

"So, I think we should have breakfast, and then we'll ke Robbie to day care, and then you and I will spend the ay together."

"Oh," she said.

"You need to work on your vocabulary, there are venty-five letters of the alphabet feeling neglected at the oment."

"Eh?"

He laughed. "How do you like your eggs? Nope, let me uess." He looked at her again, and made a big production f studying her. "Once, over easy."

"How did you know?"

"That's the only way I know how to cook them."

"Lucky me." And she meant that in every sense of the ord.

"So," he said, setting a plate in front of her, "what ould you like to do today?"

"I don't know," she whispered. Hand-holding and eye-azing sounded like a fine enough plan to her.

"How about something else you've never done before? Ve'll make it a day of firsts."

"Don't say horseback riding," she said. "I'm terrified try it."

"That's okay. That's more work than play for me.

Maybe it should be something I've never done before too."

The naughty part of her wanted to say, well, that rule out sex. Instead, she said, "I've never been swimming in the ocean."

"I don't wear shorts."

"What?"

"White legs. One of my few vanities. I spend too much time in jeans."

She burst out laughing. "Go carts, then?"

"I confess. I've done that dozens of times."

"Oh," she said suddenly, her eyes round. "Kites. On the beach. There always seems to be somebody flying those in Miracle Harbor." Hadn't Abby told her one of her most romantic moments with Shane had involved the beach and a kite?

"Perfect. Don't tell him," he said, nodding at the little boy toddling sleepily toward them, "Or he won't want to go to day care."

"Well, maybe we should include—" she said.

"No." This said so firmly, it made a shiver go up and down her spine.

"Is my donkey back?" Robbie asked.

"Yup."

"I knew you'd find him, Auntie. What day is it?"

"Thursday."

"Can I go to day care today? Nicky always goes on Thursday."

"Gee," Matt said, waggling his eyebrows fiendishly at her, "if you insist."

Now he'd gone and done it, Matt thought. Upped the heat, thrown a little more on the table. A foolish thing to do. Crazy. Stupid.

Well, he was sleep-deprived. He couldn't be held accountable.

"I'm cleaning up," she said. "You're a wonderful cook."

"I can cook an egg, anyway. And coffee. I'm an expert in coffee." He looked longingly at the couch. "If you're going to clean up, would you mind if I just lay down for a minute?"

That way, he'd be thinking nice and clear when he came to.

"Go ahead. You can stretch out on my bed, if you want."

"The couch is fine." Not her bed. Geez, he'd barely wrapped his mind around the fact there was going to be some heavy-duty kissing going on today. He thought it would be real wise to leave her bed out of that equation.

He went and stretched out on her couch. He listened to the birds, and to her and Robbie chatter. A dish broke. That seemed to just be a fact. Things got broken around her. Far off he could hear the donkey. It didn't seem to be bothering him the way it did last night.

He shut his eyes.

Just for a minute, he'd close them, just to get himself straight. He'd never approach a green horse unless he was one hundred percent there. Never.

He thought of her in those terms. Green. Full of fear. Unbroke.

God, she would have been a good woman to stay away from. On the other hand, maybe it was God who'd located her where He had.

And maybe He had his reasons.

Maybe everything, even the hardest things, were part of a larger plan. On that deeply philosophical note he managed to do what he had not done the night before. He bored himself right to sleep.

Matt awoke to a deep silence, and the feeling he was in the wrong place. He flipped over to look at his bedside clock, not liking what the brightness of the sun was telling him what time of day it was.

And he fell right off her couch.

He picked himself up and dusted himself off, found a clock over her stove. It was eleven o'clock in the morning.

"Corrie?"

"Out here."

He stumbled out her front door. She had an easel set up and was drawing something. Her casted arm was out of the sling.

"Are you supposed to be doing that?" he asked. He looked at her. He liked looking at her. Then he looked at the picture. It appeared to be that same face that had graced her easel the first day. A lovely face. Spirited, strong, elfin. Why did he recognize it?

"Oh, why not? I'm drawing a picture, not wrestling the donkey."

"What did you do with my favorite three footer?"

"Drove him to day care. He told me how to find it."

"I'm sorry. I promised you a special day, and went to sleep. That's pretty poor performance, for a man aiming—" he stopped. *Aiming to get himself kissed silly.* "Aiming to give a lady some firsts."

"It's okay. It was a first having you here."

"What?"

"Just having you on my couch. Sleeping. That was first."

"And a thrilling one, too."

She shrugged. "I liked it."

"You did?"

"I just liked it. Having you so relaxed around me. Comfortable in my house."

"Anybody ever told you, you're a cheap date?"

She looked at him. "I've never had a date," she said softly.

"What? Come on." She had to be kidding.

"I'm scared of people, Matt. I do this thing where I push the ones I want to like me the most, the farthest away."

"Does that mean you don't like me?" His throat ached when he looked at her eyes, so huge and vulnerable. He registered the fact that she had told him that she was coming to trust him in little bits and pieces.

She laughed a little. "No. Maybe it means I'm not so scared anymore. Not of you, anyway."

He wanted to ask her what had put the fear there, but he realized when she was ready, she would tell him. And when she told him, it would mean something.

That her trust in him was complete.

It seemed to him a week ago, Corrine Parsons placing that kind of faith in him would have sent him running for cover. But somehow he was not the same person he had been a while ago, and it had something to do with her.

He wondered, suddenly, about bigger things. If he'd known her before, and if his heart and soul had recognized her right away, even before his head had kicked in.

Because he felt like he knew her, and would always know her. He felt a deep comfort with her that it seemed took years to develop with other people.

He felt he was looking his soul mate in the eye.

And he'd never felt less like running. "I'm not goin
to do anything that scares you, Corrine."

She smiled. "Everything scares me. That's why I hav
to look so tough."

"You don't look tough to me."

"I know. That's because you seem to see something i
me that no one ever saw before."

"If they didn't see it, they had to be blind."

He could see the tears forming in her eyes, and kne
he had to back off now, just a touch, just like he woul
with a young horse, don't put too much pressure on i
don't move too quickly.

"Besides," he said, "you aren't scared of flying kites.
She smiled. "No."

But they both knew it wasn't about flying kites. It wa
about seeing where these feelings would lead. Trustin;
Giving. Sharing.

It wasn't about flying that kite at all.

It was about saying yes to life.

Something he'd stopped doing when his sister died. N
consciously. He hadn't shaken his fist at God and pr
claimed he was now withdrawing from the adventure (
life.

But that's still what he had done.

He had stopped saying yes to life, and Corrine had nev
said it at all.

And suddenly he knew that's why he was here. Not
steal kisses. Not for himself at all. He'd been given a
opportunity.

To help one person who was afraid, to not be afrai
anymore.

It seemed to him, looking at Corrine, that wasn't a ligl
homework assignment. It was a life's work.

And that didn't scare him either.

"Come on," he said, "let's go fly kites."

She walked toward him, and he put his hand around her shoulder, and after just a second, she leaned into him.

He smiled.

And it seemed like he didn't stop smiling for a long time. He'd worked hard all his life. Work was his life.

He couldn't ever remember a time when he had given himself over to play. Even in high school when other kids had been having fun, he'd carried the mantle of responsibility. His folks had the spread then, and the work was never ending.

And he'd never resented it. How could you resent something you didn't question? There was work that needed to be done, and he was expected to pitch in and do his part and he had.

Marianne hadn't. Nope. More a free spirit. Run off and joined some hippie community at first opportunity. She'd come home and talked about painting gourds and swimming naked and all kinds of things that just ranged from the silly to the bizarre to him.

But he'd envied her a bit, too. Not a doubt she was having fun. As she'd matured she'd even managed to make money having fun. Those gourds she painted were works of art, and people knew it.

But then she'd gotten pregnant with Robbie. By then Matt had been pretty well established. He'd bought the place from his parents, who retired to the dryer climates of Arizona.

Marianne had come home broken, somehow. She never said who the father was, wouldn't talk about it. Some of her sunshine disappeared.

Sometimes, when he looked back at it, he thought she'
started dying that day.

But she would have liked this. Big brother spending
day on the beach, being frivolous.

He found himself telling Corrie the whole story.

And when he was done, he pulled over in front of a ki
shop right on the beach, and Corrine looked at him.

"This day is for her, then, right?"

"Right," he said.

She insisted on buying the kite.

"Then," she said stubbornly, "I can pick any one
want without being embarrassed about it if I want the mo
expensive one."

"You don't have to be embarrassed about it."

"Not if I buy it, I don't," she said stubbornly. Sh
bought a huge kite. Not what he thought of as a kite
all. He thought of kites as diamond-shaped pieces of brow
wrapping paper.

Her kite was nylon, and shaped like a large half circ
that trailed about a mile of brilliantly colored tail.

"It's going to take a hurricane to get that thing up," h
said.

"No, it's not. I believe good things can happen to me.

In minutes they were on the beach. He'd lived near th
coast of Oregon all his life and could count on the finge
of one hand the number of visits he had made to the beac

She took off her shoes and wiggled her feet in the san

He slid off his boots, and by the time he had them of
she was already down the beach, laying out the kite, i
great tail behind it.

She started to run.

There wasn't a breath of air, except the stuff she wa

tirring up. She looked lithe and happy with the kite bob-
ing along behind her.

It was obviously not a one-man job, and he went to help
er.

It seemed as though as soon as he touched the kite, the
wind began to strengthen. She held it, he ran.

And suddenly it caught on the wind, and lifted.

She was running along the beach toward him, her pant
egs rolled up, her sweater tied around her throat, laughing,
umping up and down like a kid.

He gave her the string and watched her play it out, the
ght in her face.

"What does it look like?" she asked. "A dragon?"

He thought it looked like those microscope images he'd
een of sperm, but somehow he knew complete honesty
was not what was required of him at the moment.

Besides, when he looked up at it, dancing with the wind,
hat kite looked exactly like something.

Hope.

He came and stood behind her, wrapped his arms around
er waist as she played out more string, pulled the kite
his way and that, experimented with its dance, until she
ad it bucking the wind like a young colt feeling its oats.

The wind in their faces tasted of salt.

He had never ever felt this at ease with another human
eing. This right.

He shifted, took her chin in his fingers, turned her eyes
way from the kite. And kissed her. Nothing playful this
me. Not a light touching of lips.

A claim.

He was laying a claim to her.

She wrapped her arms around his neck, pressed herself
gainst him, returned his kiss.

"Hey, your kite's gettin' away," some kid yelled at them.

He couldn't have cared less, but she laughed and pulled away from him and scampered after the kite.

It seemed to take her a year to roll up that string.

But finally she was back, and she laid the kite at their feet, looked up at him.

"Where were we?" she said huskily.

"Right here," he said, and gathered her to him, and took her lips with his.

Chapter Eight

Corrine let herself give in to the powerful pull of his arms, felt the luxurious heat that came with having her body pressed full length against his. She could feel the cut of his hard muscle where his arms were around hers, where her thigh pressed his, where bosom pressed into the rock wall of a carved chest.

She did not know if she had ever felt so completely feminine. She did not know if she had ever been so aware of how soft she was in comparison to him. How delicate she was in comparison to him. How her curves were made to mold his hard lines.

Just touching him, like this, stoked the heat.

Then he kissed her.

No preliminaries. No hand-holding or eye-gazing.

Just honest, raw, unleashed passion.

With the waves crashing in the background, sending rockets of white foam shooting over nearby rocks, she answered the quest of his lips.

Tasted them.

Gloried in them. His lips looked firm, and there was no denying the command of them, but she savored the tenderness as he enveloped her mouth with his own, the welcome, and pulsing just below that, the wanting.

It felt like she had waited her whole life for this moment. Completion. The emptiness inside her filled, the hollowness banished, the belief that good things could not and would not happen to her gone, that myth washed away with the touch of his lips.

Somewhere in her there was an awareness they were on a public beach, acting like teenagers, and she wished she could make herself care.

But she couldn't.

She'd never done this when she was a teenager. A step missed. She planned to do it with a vengeance now.

It occurred to her, the kiss wasn't going to be enough.

When she had asked him this morning, if he was going to kiss her, it had been with a certain childish innocence. But a red-blooded woman was answering the invitation she had issued. And that woman knew, her instinct, primal and old as the earth told her, kisses like this were not the end. They were the beginning.

This kiss, that stoked the heat in her to unbearable intensity, was really only the first lick of flame that could burn blue bright if she fueled it.

She realized, startled, she wanted it all. Not just his lips. Not just an innocent kiss on a public beach. She wanted to follow this trail of fire. She wanted to feel the heated silk of his naked skin under her fingertips, the whisker-roughness of his cheeks against her feverish lips. She wanted to touch the muscles that bulged so enticingly on his arms, and run her tongue down the length of that vein that throbbed, just below the skin on the inside of his arm, from the curve of his bicep to his elbow.

She wanted to feel the hard swell of his unclothed chest against the sensitive softness of her own cheeks, to lay a trail fire with her tongue from his breastbone to his belly button.

And she wanted his hands to touch her. In places she had never been touched before. She wanted to feel his lips anoint every inch of her skin, rain exquisite, torturous, tender fire on her.

Obviously, even in the throes of her newfound delight and desire, she wasn't about to go any further on a beach.

"Let's go home," she whispered huskily.

He gently put her away from him, studied her, teased a tendril of hair back from her face with his finger.

"Are you sure?"

She nodded, her throat dry, her eyes aching with unshed emotion, her skin tingling, her heart trembling.

He leaned forward, kissed her on the tip of her nose. He scooped the kite out of the sand with one hand, wrapped the other over her shoulder.

They walked through the sand, and she felt a sense of being a part of something. She had felt the sense of being a part of something for the first time when she had met her sisters.

But this sensation was different. Far different. She and her sisters had become a circle of three. A family.

But with him, she was a part of a twosome. A couple.

That was it. She felt like she was part of a couple. How often had she watched romantic pairs, pretending not to watch, the envy veiled in her eyes? They were everywhere, on summer beaches, and strolling through autumn leaves, those lovers who had only eyes for each other.

Who didn't even know she watched as they walked, laughing, or silent, or conversing with the quiet intensity

of people who truly knew each other. The gift of their
intimacy singing around them.

Always connected in some way physically. Their hands
touching, or his hand over her shoulder, possessively, pro-
tectively, her arm around his waist, at home there, as if it
belonged there. He might reach over and nip her ear with
his teeth, or bury his nose in her neck, or she might reach
up to laughingly dislodge a leaf from his hair.

Connected in some way less concrete, held together by
the invisible threads of love, that showed in the way their
heads were close together as they shared some secret or
discussed where they were going for dinner.

Corrine had always felt excluded from these intimacies.
An outsider. The one who had never been included.

And now, just like that, she was on the inside, looking
out.

His arm was draped over her shoulders, dragging their
kite along behind them, his eyes on her, full of wonder,
reverence and stunned discovery—things she knew were
reflected in her own eyes.

That look. *I have found what I was looking for.*

Somehow, without a map, without even knowing most
days what she was looking for, she had found it anyway,
or it had found her.

They stopped and sat in the sand beside their shoes. He
took her ankle in his hand, and brushed the sand from the
bottoms of her feet. His hand was hard and smooth, like
leather, and the sensuality of the tiny gesture was so intense she wanted to grab her foot away.

It was shockingly sexy, almost more so than the kiss.

He looked at her expression, grinned wickedly, and began to make slow circles in the arch of her foot with his
thumb, his eyes darkened with knowing, never leaving her
face.

She yanked her foot away before she embarrassed her-
lf by moaning with animal-like pleading, pleasure and
ain.

Blushing, her head ducked, she fumbled with her socks,
e laces of her sneakers. She couldn't bring herself to
ven look at his feet, let alone brush the sand off of them.
he desire was raging in her, so hot it felt like she was
oing to be turned to ash.

And that possibility would not stop her.

It seemed nothing could stop her. They had come to that
ace.

To a place where only one option was left, complete
rrender. She closed her eyes, willing herself to be re-
rned to sanity, but instead she could see them in the
ngle of her sheets, his body covering hers.

He helped her to her feet, but she could see the urgency
him now, too.

They had just reached his truck, when Corrine caught a
rst of color out of the corner of her eye.

"Corrie!"

She turned to see Brit charging out of her bakery, com-
g toward them.

"I've been calling you all day," she said breathlessly.
Where have you been?"

Corrine tried to think of an answer more circumspect
an *kissing like a house on fire on the beach.*

Thankfully, because Corrine's mind was moving with a
uggish, dream-like quality, Brit didn't seem to be waiting
r an answer.

"Angela Pondergrove has been in an accident."

Corrine, just barely, could place Angela from her sisters'
eddings. A sweet little old lady. Oh, yes, who gave away
edding outfits.

Who knew their mother. Who had answers.

"We've been waiting for her to get home. Remember? So we could talk to her?"

She did remember now, clearly. She felt herself reluctantly leaving that place she had shared with Matt, reentering the world at Main Street, Miracle Harbor.

Not a bad place. Had it always been this bright? As everything on it shone with an inner light?

"Angela is in Minnesota. It looks really bad. Poor Jordan is just beside himself. Mitch is sick with worrying about him."

Corrine finally succeeded in completely dragging her drugged brain away from the pulsating presence of the man at her side.

"Minnesota?" she said.

"Mitch has arranged a flight. For this afternoon. I was having a bird when I couldn't find you. I even drove out to your place, and your car was still there, so I called and called."

And here she'd been cavorting on the beach right before her sister's eyes.

"But why did you need to find me?" Corrine asked, "I mean, I'm sorry. And I'm really sorry about Mitch's dad being so upset, but what does it have to do with me?"

"Angela's asked us to come. She wants to talk to us about our mother."

Corrine thought it was a mark of how upset her sister was that she seemed to have barely registered the man at her sister's side.

"The flight leaves in an hour," Brit said.

Corrine felt as if her whole world was dissolving. The thing she had wanted most taken from her, as always.

"That hardly even gives me time to go home and pack," Corrine said.

"Lucky for you, you have sisters exactly the same size

ust the excuse I've been looking for to do something
bout your wardrobe.''

Suddenly Brit's eyes went very round as if she just re-
lized her sister wasn't alone. "Oh, hello, Matt.''

He nodded, but his attention was completely focused on
orrine. "You have to go,'' he said firmly. He leaned
lose to her and said, "I'll be here when you get back.
ou know that.''

But she didn't.

She felt a nameless panic, as if once again her life had
een wrested from her control. She had just started to like
place, to believe, and the rug was pulled out from under
er. It was a repeat of her horrid experiences with the
oster-care system.

She was the one who had made the mistake. Believing.
loping. Trusting.

Why was Angela in Minnesota, for God's sake? The
ery place Corrine had left behind? She knew why. Be-
ause that was where the story had started. A woman had
ied and for some reason her triplet daughters had been
eparated.

And Angela had to know that reason. And so did Cor-
ne.

She had to know it even more than she had to go back
o her cabin with Matt. Because somehow it seemed to her
ne whole future was linked to that shadowy past.

Until she came to terms with that, had answers to *why*
ne was the child who had been cast away, she could not
ave a future.

No matter how hard she tried to wish and believe and
ust, she had to go back there. She wished, foolishly, he
ould come with her.

She sought the calm of his eyes. The steady strength of

them. She wanted him to come, to shield her and protect her and hold her.

She could not ask. How could she ask him that? He had his nephew and his ranch to look after.

He hardly knew her.

A shocking admission, that they hardly knew each other. But those were the facts.

Even if her heart and soul cried that she had known him forever, the facts spoke differently.

"I'll look after the donkey," he said.

That much had changed, at least. She'd never had anything to leave behind before. Or anything to come back to.

She looked at him standing there, so strong, and patient and sure.

Sure she was coming back.

Sure that he would be here.

What made a person so confident that life would unfold just as they thought it would? He had experienced hard knocks, too. Why had he weathered them so much better than she had? Some faith in life still there in the unflinching calm of his eyes.

He leaned forward, and kissed her hard, on the mouth.

And some of his certainty passed to her. He seemed to be saying it would be all right. Telling her to have courage.

By kissing her in front of her sister, it was like he was committing to something.

Something that looked suspiciously like the future.

He broke away from her. They stood looking at each other.

"Look, you know I'd be the last one to break up a moment like this," Brit said regretfully. "But we have a plane we have to be on."

He stepped back.

So did she. She half lifted her hand in farewell, and he took it, lifted it to his lips, his eyes locked on hers. He kissed her hand.

It was the most tender moment Corrine had ever experienced.

Her mouth fell open, and tears pressed behind her eyes.

Her sister took her and propelled her away, but Corrine kept glancing over her shoulder at him, even after he had turned away, and put the kite in the truck, and started the engine.

She saw him glance at her, shove the truck into gear.

She was not sure if he saw her put her hand to her lips, kiss her fingertips, and blow all her hopes and dreams after that departing truck.

"It looks like exciting developments in the romance department," Brit breathed. "My God, I could fry doughnuts in the sizzle between the two of you."

It already felt like it was disappearing. Going, going, gone.

Because sizzle was different than love. It was exactly like what it sounded like—a flash in the pan. Red-hot flames leaving nothing but ash.

"I don't want to talk about it," Corrine said, and hated the look of hurt she had caused to come onto her sister's beautiful face.

She wondered why it was so easy for her to see her sister's beauty, and not to see her own.

Matt drove away, shocked to see his hands trembling on the steering wheel. Desire thwarted.

Shocked, really at how he had behaved.

A grown man acting like a teenage boy on the beach. Still, there was no regret. No, not true. One regret.

He'd wanted to say he'd go with her.

Face whatever dragons haunted her. He'd seen thos
dragons reflected in her face as soon as her sister had tol
her they needed to go to Minnesota.

How he wanted to go and slay that dragon for her.

But how could he? He had responsibilities. Robbie. Th
ranch. Even her donkey had become his responsibility.

It was a good thing she was gone, he told himse
roughly. Things were moving way too fast.

The universe had imposed a speed limit. A speed bum
maybe. Slowed them down. He needed time to think.

He was a man firing on only one barrel at the momen
Sleep deprived. Intoxicated with the feelings she caused i
him.

Lust, he told himself.

And felt some strange happiness unfurl in him, when h
knew, absolutely and without a doubt that what he felt fo
Corrine Parsons was a hell of a lot more than lust.

After all, he knew lust. What man didn't?

And this went deeper and further and harder.

Maybe it was even the other L-word.

Love.

How could he love her? He'd known her only a matt
of weeks.

Then again, he'd known Barbara for years. And it wa
only now, now that he had something to compare to, th
he realized how shallow his feelings for her had run.

And Robbie? He had loved Robbie from the first secon
of the child's life. Deeply. Abidingly.

A man could be on the planet a long, long time, an
not understand that simple four letter word. Love.

But the feelings.

Of wanting to be with her. Of wanting to know every
thing about her. Of wanting to please her and protect he

Of wanting to be the one who chased the fear from her eyes for good.

Of wanting to laugh with her into old age. And kiss her hands, and run his lips along the arch of her foot until she was limp with wanting.

Of wanting her to be the best she could be, to leave her insecurities behind her and find in his love the foundation she needed to spring forward into her fullness as a human being.

Of wanting her to be the one he trusted his heart to. And the one who carried his babies. And the one who cradled his head when he was tired, and took him to places within himself he had never known he could go.

Places within himself that showed how far a man could grow.

A man could be more than a working fool. More than his job. More than his house and his property.

He could become something more than he had ever dreamed. If he said yes when this feeling came knocking on his door. If he said yes, instead of running the other way.

He wanted to take it to the limit with her—and then find out he didn't even know what the limits were. That whole world awaited him. Places of spirit and soul that he had never traveled before, places that love opened the door to.

He was scared to death, and not scared at all, at the very same time.

He glanced at his watch, and laughed.

Mrs. Beatle would be mad again. Furious with him. Frustrated. And being in love even changed that. Because he knew why she focused so intently on the small things.

Because somewhere along the way, Mrs. Beatle had said no to the biggest thing.

The biggest thing of all.

                         *   *   *

Corrine thought Mrs. Pondergrove looked small and terribly frail in the hospital bed. She felt herself draw behind
her sisters, scared to be here.

She wanted to have the mysteries of her life solved, and
wanted nothing less.

Mrs. Pondergrove opened her eyes, and the twinkle in
them made Corrine think of youth instead of age.

"Oh, girls," she said, "how lovely of you to come.
What a terrible thing. This isn't how I planned it at all. I
wanted to tell you everything after Corrine's wedding, of
course, but now I feel this terrible urgency. I know the
doctors have said I will be fine, but I don't feel like that."

Corrine's wedding? Corrine felt startled. She wasn't
getting married.

"Don't even say that, Angela," Jordan Hamilton said,
coming forward, taking her hand. "You are going to be
fine. Do you hear me?"

"Oh, Jordan," she said with a smile, "we're too old for
such nonsense. I don't believe I have enough energy left
for a romance, even if I do ever get out of here."

"Well, you had enough energy to drive yourself halfway across the continent, so I would think a little romance
would be nothing to you."

"You mustn't scold me anymore. Especially not in front
of the girls. I think they came to hear what I have to say.
Didn't you?"

Jordan turned and glared at them.

Abby and Corrine got it and remained silent, but Brit,
oblivious as always, said, "I certainly did. I've really never
quite forgiven you for dropping that bombshell that you
knew our mother. Why did you disappear right after that?"

"Oh, dear. You have far more to forgive me for than

at. Pull up some chairs, young ladies. I'm afraid you are going to be here for a while.''

''Don't you tire yourself out,'' Jordan said. He looked at Abby, obviously having picked out the most sensible one. ''If you see her wearing out—''

''I promise,'' Abby said gently, and watched him leave the room, smiling. She pulled up a chair, and took Angela's hand and stroked it.

Corrine thought it was such a lovely thing to do. The kind of gesture she never could have managed with any sincerity.

''Angela,'' Abby said, ''that man is in love with you. You're not going to break his heart are you?''

''Oh, dear, I already have so much on my conscience, there really isn't room for anymore.''

''Do you really feel like you're dying?'' Brit asked bluntly.

''I do,'' Angela said softly. ''There's this weight in me that won't go away. A heaviness of spirit.''

The sisters sat there silently, contemplating that.

Angela began to speak, her voice soft and weak and faraway. ''It was twenty-four years ago that I was last here. In the winter. Corrine, dear, you know Minnesota in the winter?''

''And how,'' Corrine said, both sorry and pleased to have been singled out.

''I didn't. I was accompanying my husband on one of his business trips. He loved to drive. And I loved being with him. Nothing made me happier than that man. I know what love does to people. How it makes them so alive, and so in love with life. I know because I had it once.

''Dear Alf, gone nine years now. He left a fortune. Was saving it for our retirement. He wanted to go around the world. Cruise ships. Greece. The Caribbean. The class act,

he was going to give me. Silly man. As if he didn't give
me the class act every single day that he breathed in and
out. I tell people now to spend it if they have it. Don'
save it for a day that may never come.

"No wonder Mitch calls me meddlesome," she continued, her eyes smiling at Brittany. "I just can't seem to
mind my own business anymore.

"Which brings me back to you, to how my life is linked
with each of yours. That blizzard just came out of no
where. I had never seen anything like that. One minute the
skies were crystal blue and clear, and the next, the huge
white cloud that had been hovering in the distance was
right on top of us. The horizon melted into the sky. The
visibility was so terrible, it felt like we had jumped into a
vat full of white feathers. We literally could not see the
road in front of us. We couldn't even pull off the road, fo
fear that if we stopped we would be hit.

"We started to pass dreadful things. Cars in the ditch
Flipped over. A trailer truck jackknifed. The roads had
turned into ice rinks. I could see Alf sweating, his hands
white on the steering wheel, leaning up close to the wind
shield as if somehow that would help him see.

"And then he cried out, and I saw we were way too
close to the vehicle in front of us."

She stopped, and her voice faraway, she said, "It's
funny when you get old. I can remember every detail of
that afternoon twenty-four years ago. I can remember what
I was wearing, and what Alf was wearing, and the scen
of the air freshener that hung on our mirror. But I can'
remember what I had for lunch today."

She stopped and drew a deep and shuddering breath.

"Angela, don't tell it, if it's going to upset you," Abby
said.

"It's upset me for twenty-four years. Ruled me. Maybe elling it will finally bring me the peace I need. To go on."

The sisters exchanged worried glances.

"Our car was sliding, and by some miracle we didn't it the vehicle in front of us, we slid right around it. I was ;rabbing the front dash, looking straight ahead and I saw vhat happened next. First, only out of the corner of my ·ye, unfolding like it was in slow motion.

"It was a blue car. A small one, like a young family lrives. A truck had turned sideways in front of it. A big, vhite panel truck.

"I can still see the black letters on the side. Herb's ·xterminating. And a picture of a spider. A huge black pider, with hairy legs, and red eyes."

The picture flashed through Corrie's mind, not as if she vas trying to imagine it. No, as if she was remembering t. She felt suddenly faint.

"Are you all right, dear?" Angela asked.

She shook her head, mutely, silent tears flowing down ter cheeks. Brit and Abby pulled their chairs closer, cud-lled her, took her cold hands in theirs.

"I remember that," she whispered. "I remember that ·icture. That's why we're so afraid of spiders."

Angela nodded, her tears joining Corrine's. "Yes, dear, hat's why."

Brit stood up. "I'm just going to get Corrie a coffee. Abby, you want one? Mrs. Pondergrove?"

Abby shook her head, and Angela Pondergrove seemed o have turned inward, as if she was on an icy road twenty-our years ago reliving a nightmare.

Brit came back, and Corrine felt her unfold her own icy ingers and stick the cardboard cup in her hands.

"Are you all right, dear?" Mrs. Pondergrove asked.

Corrine nodded, not trusting her voice.

"I saw the man's face, the one driving the little blue car. He was so young, and handsome. He had this look on his face. Not fear. Grim determination. But of course there was nothing he could do. The little car hit the truck," Mrs. Pondergrove whispered, "and dissolved. There were parts of it flying everywhere.

"We slid in front of the truck, and then Alf pulled off the road, or at least he hoped he was off the road, and he opened his door and ran out into the blizzard.

"I knew he was going back to that little blue car. I'm so ashamed to say how scared I was, how much I didn't want to go. But I did. I forced myself to get out of the car and go back to that accident.

"The man, the man who had been driving that car was dead. I'd never seen a dead person before, but somehow you know that dreadful fact when there comes a time you have to know it. He'd been thrown clear. And then I saw a woman, in a snowdrift, a brightness in all that snow. I heard her crying, and I wasn't afraid anymore.

"I went to her. And got down in the snow right beside her, and when I saw she was shivering I took off my coat and put it over her. And I never even felt the cold.

"All around me were sounds. Cars skidding on the ice, and hitting each other, but no sounds of sirens. It would be a long time before the ambulances could get through on those roads.

"For all that chaos, for all that noise, it seemed like it was just me and her. Oh my, she was beautiful. She had this hair that was as golden as a halo, and eyes that were astonishing. I had never seen eyes quite that hazel, not that is, until I saw you.

"I knew she was dying. I could see it in her eyes, almost smell it in the air around her, feel it coming to get her."

Corrine saw both her sisters were crying now.

"And I knew I had been given a most special honor. That it was my job, somehow, to make her passing as painless as I could. To hold her hand, and stroke her hair, and listen to her, and surround her with love. To keep her calm in any way I could.

"And that's what I did. I listened to her. I made her the promise that brought her peace. After I made her that promise, she smiled, oh, the most radiant smile. I can still feel it today, right in my soul. She squeezed my hand, and she was gone.

"And then I heard the babies crying."

Chapter Nine

"It was when I heard the babies cry, that I remember the look on that young man's face. Not of fear, but determination. Determination to save his babies." Angela leaned against the pillows, and looked suddenly exhausted. "I'm very tired. I'm so sorry."

"That's enough for one day," Abby said firmly. "You don't have to tell us anymore right now."

"Yes, dear, I do. I have to tell you all of it. And especially the promise I made to your mother. And didn't keep. Couldn't keep."

"It will hold until tomorrow," Abby said as Brit went out of the room and came back with Jordan.

They all watched him, as he came into the room. Tall, silver-haired, distinguished, he took in Angela's expression, and rushed to her side. Without the slightest hesitation, he slid her over in the bed, and climbed up on beside her in his impeccable suit. He gathered her to him, and Corrine watched her relax, smile slightly, reach up and

ver his hand with hers. It was as if, suddenly, they were
e only two people in the world.

It reminded her so painfully of Matt. And of what she
inted.

Jordan had arranged for them to have rooms at a hotel
ar the hospital. Abby and Brit wanted to go out for din-
r, but Corrine begged off. After the hotel room door had
osed behind them, she took the keys for the rental car
d left, leaving her sisters a note telling them she had
ne for a drive.

A silly thing to do, drive from Minneapolis out to St.
oud, and past all her terrible memories. Her Aunt Ella's
iall grim looking house, each of the foster homes.

Back in Minneapolis, a drive by her old apartment build-
g even made her feel as though her whole life had been
ipty and incomplete.

It was as if Minnesota had wounded her. And by going
vay the wound had started to heal.

But driving around that night, she pulled the scab away.
id she felt that belief that she had been holding so tight
that good things could happen to her, falter inside of
r.

Why should they? They never had before. By coming
ck here she had been plunged back into what she had
en. It was like coming from a warm bath and diving into
icy lake.

"Where did you go?" her sisters asked worriedly when
e finally went back to the hotel.

She smiled as if nothing had changed. "Reality check,"
e said, and that was all.

In the morning they went back to see Angela.

The old woman looked decidedly more chipper this
orning. She invited them all to sit down, and picked up

the threads of her story. "I feel so much better this morning. Are you ready to continue?"

Her sisters seemed eager to hear the rest of the story
but Corrine felt reluctance in her nod.

"Her name was Belle, that beautiful young woman who
died on the highway that day. Abby, you named your
daughter after her. I like to think that some part of you
remembered her as love and joy, and so when that great
love and joy came to your life you knew what to call it.

"For the small time I spent with her, that was the impression I got. That your mother was a woman who was
able to do the rarest of things, combine gentleness with
strength.

"At first she talked about her husband, Allan. I don't
know if she knew he had already died, and I didn't tell
her. She talked about the love they had found, and how
rare it was, how they had fallen in love so quickly that
nobody had ever thought it would work. And how her love
for him—and his for her—had brought her as close to
heaven as she felt a person was allowed to come on this
earth.

"Don't you think it's remarkable that you girls have all
had whirlwind courtships, too?"

Abby and Brit nodded. Corrine said nothing.

"And then she talked about you. Her three babies. They
named you in the order you were born, with letters of the
alphabet—Abigail, Brittany and Corrine. She talked about
the delight you brought them, because they had almost
given up on having children. You were their miracle.

"She was so worried about not being there to help you
grow up. So worried about missing all the wonderful
events of your lives, your first day at school, and your
graduations, and your weddings. She was so worried when

ould teach you how to love now that she was going
way.''

Corrine wanted to bury her head in her hands and sob,
ut it seemed she had remembered the rules all over again.
nd the first one was never to cry.

She felt Abby touch her shoulder, her hand lingering
ere.

''They didn't have an extended family, Belle and Allan.
here was only one other sister, your mother's sister. I
on't remember her name now.''

''Ella Bigelow,'' Corrine whispered. ''Auntie Ella.''

''Ah, yes. Belle was so frightened about her girls going
 her sister. She loved her sister, but she said she was
agile emotionally. That she would never be able to give
ou girls what Belle wanted for you—a home full of love
id warmth and hugs and kisses, where muddy feet didn't
atter and jam smears were the order of the day.

''Funny, to remember it so clearly.'' Angela sighed. ''I
in hear her voice, like she's right here beside me.

''She was becoming quite agitated, worrying about you
rls going to Ella. Whatever strength she had left in her
ie squeezed into my hand. And she made me promise,''
ngela's voice caught, and then she swallowed, and went
1. ''She made me promise I would make sure you were
appy. That I would do what I could to look after you.
nd I promised her that. On a frozen winter night in the
iddle of a nightmare on a road between St. Cloud and
ittle Falls, Minnesota, I made a promise to your mother.''

Angela was crying, and so were Brit and Abby. But
orrine's tears were frozen, some wall that she had nearly
roken down, being slammed back up.

''I didn't keep my promise,'' Angela sobbed. ''I didn't
10w how. I wasn't family. I couldn't even get information
)out the three of you from the hospital. That evening, I

heard on the news, like everyone else, that you all ha
lived. How could I influence what happened to you next

"We were back on the road as soon as the stor
cleared. Alf had to be at a conference in Ontario, and w
just moved on.

"But I never really moved on. I had left a part of m
soul back there on that road when I made that promise
And how I would fret over the years, wondering what ha
happened to those three tiny children cut from that car tha
night, children I had promised to look after. Alf, bless hi
soul, saw how much pain it caused me, and he just wante
me to forget about it.

"But when he died, and I saw all that money, it seeme
to me maybe I had the means to finally make good on tha
promise. I hired a detective to find you, and to find ou
what had happened to each of you. I was devastated b
the news he brought me. That you had been split up.

"Corrine, you were the first one released from the hos
pital. Amazingly you just had a few bruises and scratches
Your aunt Ella took you home. I can't condemn her, bu
your mother knew her weaknesses. As far as we coul
piece together, she found one three-year-old more than sh
could handle.

"Meanwhile, at the hospital, a nurse named Judy Blake
ly had been looking after Abby, who was in critical con
dition. She nursed her back to health, and she fell in lov
with her. She couldn't bear to let her go.

"By the time she approached Ella, Ella had had Corrin
two months. She must have known by then she was i
over her head. That she was barely coping with one chilc
What was she going to do with one more? And then tw
more? I think she was relieved when Judy asked her abou
adopting Abby. A lawyer was involved, and I feel the sec
ond adoption, Brittany's, may have been at his instigatior

We're fairly certain money changed hands before Brittany was adopted by Conroy and Michelle Patterson in California.''

''I knew it!'' Brittany said.

''But if she wasn't coping why didn't she put me up for adoption, too?'' Corrine asked, finding the pain and bewilderment in her own voice pathetic, despising herself for being so weak, for caring so much.

''That's a question we'll never know the answer to, my dear. Abby and Brittany, your aunt Ella died about sixteen years ago.''

''But that would have meant Corrine was only eleven years old. What happened to her?''

''I think it's up to Corrine to tell you, if she wants to.''

Corrine didn't want to. She looked everywhere but into the sympathy-laden eyes of her sisters. ''By the time I was six, Aunt Ella was in la-la land on a pretty regular basis. I started going to foster homes when she had her episodes.''

In the silence, her sisters watched her, not knowing the softness in their eyes was killing her, filling her with a desperate need to have things she couldn't ever have now.

That was the mistake she had made. She couldn't ever be brand-new, no matter how hard she tried.

She was not bringing this mess that she was to Matt. And Robbie. They would be better off without her.

''And when she died? Couldn't somebody have adopted you then?'' Abby asked, tears leaving salty trails on her cheeks.

''Nobody wanted to,'' Corrine whispered. The word *incorrigible* had been stamped across her forehead. Grief and confusion became anger and rebellion in the hostile silence that followed.

''I can't believe my mother—Judy—did this to me,''

Abby said, with the closest thing to real fury in her voice Corrine had ever heard. "She knew. How could she keep me from my sisters? From Corrine. Corrine needed us."

Something inside Corrine was freezing solid. Scream ing. *No, I didn't need you. I didn't need anyone.*

It felt like if she admitted the enormity of that lie, the depth of her desire to need someone, to be needed, she would die. Just lay down and die of a broken heart.

"Judy Blakely had problems of her own, I think," An gela said, gently. "Family difficulties that forced her move to Chicago. Your aunt Ella was a difficult person. She may not have encouraged Judy to keep in touch."

"Did my parents know?" Brit asked. "About the othe two?"

"I think you'll have to ask your parents that. Anyway to finish my tale, I had the private detective track you down, to assuage my own feelings of guilt. I wanted him to find you all happy and well adjusted and raising familie of your own.

"But instead the scars of that dreadful night seemed to have reached into the future. Abby was alone with a baby Brittany couldn't grow up. And our poor Corrine."

Don't, Corrine seethed silently, *don't you dare feel sorr for me.*

"I gave you the gifts," Angela whispered. "Abby the gift of security. Brittany the gift of responsibility. And what did you need most, Corrine?"

"You sent the donkey," she guessed. But she couldn' admit knowing the real gift. *What I needed most was some thing to care about.* Only that something had become so much more. Matt and Robbie.

God. It was all part of a plan. Angela's plan. She thought of her sisters meeting those men. Shane *acciden tally* living in the same house Abby had inherited. Mitch being Jordan's adopted son.

"I put in the part about getting married because I had known such joy as a married woman and so had your mother. It seemed to me your joy, each of you, lay in the place you were most trying to avoid."

All her life people had made plans for her. Told her what would be best for her. She had never had the freedom to make choices.

She had been manipulated into caring about her neighbor.

But why had he cared back? Or did he? Maybe that was the biggest joke of all. That a man like Matt Donahue would genuinely care about a woman like her.

"You knew Matt wanted that land back, didn't you?" Corrine whispered. How had she managed to forget that little fact? Dismiss it? That he wanted his land back.

What length was he willing to go to, to get it?

Probably any length. Any length, at all. She was incorrigible and unwanted. What a fool she had been to think that had changed.

It was just a silly old woman playing with her life.

"After I told you girls I knew your mother," Angela said softly, "just before Brit's wedding, I began to doubt what I was doing. I mean, I loved how it was working out, but it suddenly seemed to me I was playing God, and I felt so foolish, and unsure. I needed some time to myself, to think. So I began to drive, and then I knew where I was driving.

"Back to that place. That stretch of road. I found your mother's grave, and it brought me great comfort, being with her. I brought her flowers every day, and just stayed and talked. About life, and my own confusion.

"It was on the way back from one of those talks that I

had my accident, and knew I had to tell you the whole truth before I died.''

''You are not going to die,'' Abby said firmly.

Corrine felt like she was watching them from a long distance away. She had the most terrible sensation that none of it was real.

The past few weeks of her life just going according to a script that someone else had written.

They knew now. Her sisters knew no one had ever loved her. No one had ever wanted her.

She knew what would happen next. They would start looking at her out of the corners of their eyes, and they would see what she was really like. That she was uncommunicative and surly and introverted. That she wasn't a nice person at all, like they were.

And Matt would see it, too. How long would she have been able to keep up the charade that she was wholesome and laughter-filled? How long before the shadows crept back and everyone discovered that she had never learned how to love people?

She had nothing to give.

And she could not hurt her sisters with that. Or Matt and Robbie. Or even Angela.

Pathetic as it was, she was glad she still had her donkey. He would never expect anything of her beyond a daily feeding, a scratch on his brow.

She knew what she was going to do. She was going to go get her donkey, and go. Somewhere she had never been before. Somewhere where no one knew her or expected her to be all the things she would never, ever be: warm and loving and full of fun.

The kind of woman who could run with wild abandon across sand with a kite dancing on the air behind her.

The kind of woman who could kiss a man like that in public.

She got up. They had still been talking, and she was aware she had interrupted but she didn't quite know what.

"I'm not feeling well," she said. "I'm going to walk back to the hotel."

"I'll drive you," Abby said, leaping to her feet.

She savored that. Her last moment with her sister. Her sister caring about her so much.

"No. I need to walk. I need the fresh air."

Abby was going to hug her. It felt like it would destroy her. She backed quickly away, turned on her heel and walked out the door.

Love was just too hard. It asked to much. It asked a person to be vulnerable and open, and she couldn't be those things.

Corrine began to run.

"What do you mean, your sister is gone?" Matt asked, trying to shake the sleep from his head. He had barely slept a wink since she had left. The donkey seemed to miss her. He brayed nonstop. Matt could hear him clearly all the way at his house.

Tonight, Matt had given in. He'd loaded Cupie Doll in the trailer and hauled her down to Corrine's, and with Robbie cheering him on, he let her go in the newly repaired pasture.

And then he let the donkey out.

Cupie Doll was infertile, anyway, and bloody miserable about it. Except that the vet had told him a donkey's semen was stronger than a horse's. A mare who had not taken with a stud often came around for a donkey.

Imagine being able to learn new things at his age.

He and Robbie had watched them chase around that

pasture, not even trying a fence. He'd managed to get Robbie out of there before the action really started.

Mrs. Beatle would probably not approve of Robbie recounting *that* to his playground chums.

He tried again to come fully awake.

The woman on the other end of the line might be crying. Which sister? *B*. Bonnie? Bethany. Brit. That was it. Brittany.

It struck him suddenly, what she was saying. "Corrine's missing?" he said.

Now he was awake, listening with everything he had. He hung up the phone and contemplated the wall.

Obey your first instinct.

He should have gone with her. Plain and simple.

Obviously, she wasn't lost. She was twenty-seven years old, in the city she'd been born in. She wasn't lost. She just didn't want to be found.

Brittany had asked him to call if he heard from Corrie. He'd jotted down the number she gave him, even though he knew he wasn't going to hear from her.

She was pulling up stakes.

Brittany hadn't told him the whole story, but enough. A crazy aunt. Foster homes, no hope of adoption.

It always came to this, with a frightened thing. There came a turning point. And a choice. To turn toward you, or to run away.

Corrine had made her choice.

But he had a sudden hunch that she'd come back for the donkey. And that was the only other thing he knew for certain about taking on something frightened and wild and hoping to tame it. At some point you just had to throw the rule book away and go where there were no rules.

You had to go to that place your heart told you to go. And his heart told him she was coming back for that

onkey. He sat on the edge of his bed, gave his head a
nake, and reached for his jeans.

He went into Robbie's room, and pulled the blankets
ut from where they were tucked into the mattress,
rapped them around Robbie and gathered him in his
rms. Robbie had a book in his hand, and when it fell to
he floor, he woke and cried out.

"Brandy. I need Brandy."

Matt stooped and picked up the book, stared at it. It was
he book Robbie insisted they read over and over again.
he drawing on the cover was very similar to the one he
ad seen on the easel in Corrine's living room.

"Give it to me, Auntie."

"Go back to sleep. We have to go to Corrine's."

"Is she home?" Robbie asked eagerly, coming a little
ore awake.

"Not yet."

"Do you know who she really is?" he whispered to
Matt.

"Yeah, I think so."

"She's Brandy," Robbie told him groggily, and took
he book back, tucked it under his arm. He put his thumb
n his mouth and rested his head on his uncle's shoulder.
I prayed for her to come."

"Why?" Matt whispered.

"Because she knew how much it hurt inside."

"Her and the donkey, eh, sport?"

"Yeah."

"How come you didn't tell me?"

"My mommy told me to look after you. I wasn't sure
ow. That's why I prayed for Brandy to come. She knows
verything."

It was coming back to him now, his nephew's attach-

ment to the book about the spunky little orphan girl who
got herself in and out of pickles with amazing heart.

He frowned. Somebody had given him that book.
Pressed it into his hand at Marianne's funeral. A little old
lady he hadn't known. He'd assumed she knew Marianne.

If the sister called back he was asking what Angela Pondergrove looked like.

Robbie snuggled deeper into his shoulder, and he put
him in the truck, started it and went down the hill.

He was afraid she might have been already, might have
come back at lightning speed, taken the donkey and left.

But the donkey and old Cupie Doll were munching grass
side by side in the moonlight.

He picked up Robbie and went up the stairs, deftly
avoiding the second one. Her door was locked, but he
knew the lock, and it was a flimsy one.

He only felt a moment of guilt when he gave a well-
placed kick above the latch, and the door popped open.

He went and put Robbie on her couch, and when he was
sleeping he pried the book from his hand.

Brandy, written and illustrated by Corrine Parsons. No
picture of the author, or he knew he would have recognized her.

Funny, how he didn't need a picture to recognize her
now. Corrine was in every line. Finally, she was telling
him about all those hurt places. But more, she was telling
him about her heart.

Her wonderful brave, strong, invincible heart coming
alive in this character she had created.

After awhile, he kicked off his boots and tilted his head
back against the top of her sofa. And fell asleep.

He awoke to the sound of a car door slamming, and
bolted up right. He went on stocking feet to the window
and saw her paying the cab driver. He turned from the

window, heard her soft intake of breath when she found the open door.

Hadn't she seen his truck?

"Is somebody there?" Her voice as full of fear as her eyes had been that first day.

"I am," he called softly. "I'm here, Corrine."

The light snapped on, and he had to shield his eyes from the sudden brilliance.

"What are you doing here?" she snapped.

"I thought you and I had some unfinished business."

"Well, we don't. You can have your land. And you don't even have to marry me for it."

"You lost me somewhere along the way, there, sugar."

"Sure, I did. Get out of my house."

Instead he folded his arms over his chest. No fast moves now. Just soft and sweet and gentle. "Your sisters called me. They were worried about you."

"They don't have to worry about me anymore."

"Why's that, Corrine?"

"They just don't."

She stomped by him, and hauled a suitcase out of her bedroom. She snapped open the lid and began throwing things in.

"Are you going somewhere?" he asked.

"As a matter of fact, I am."

"Where?"

"Anywhere you aren't."

"What are you so scared of?"

She stiffened, straightened and looked at him with regal dislike. "I am not afraid of anything."

"Yes, you are. You're afraid of everything. You know most people are afraid of dying. But not you. No sir. You are afraid of living."

"Where can I rent a horse trailer?" she asked.

Aha. She'd come back for the donkey. A rude, stubborn ugly animal. Which Matt took to mean there might be faint hope for him.

"Why would you want a horse trailer? You don't have a horse."

"You know why I want a horse trailer."

"Where are you going to go, Corrine?" he asked softly. He noticed Robbie stir restlessly, wondered for an uneasy moment if his nephew was awake.

"Somewhere where not a soul knows me."

"You know the problem? You can go anywhere you want, but you can't escape yourself."

She glared at him.

"Besides, you can't go anywhere."

"Why not?"

"Because your donkey has been on my mare. There might be a paternity suit." He decided now wouldn't be the best time to tell her his mare was out in her pasture at the moment. Voluntarily.

She looked so tired. And like she was fighting so hard to control herself. He wanted to go and hold her, to tell her it was safe here.

That he was a safe guy to give her heart to.

But he knew that wasn't something you could tell people. They had to decide it all by themselves. If he could just buy a few days. Let her get over whatever had happened to her in Minneapolis. Tell him about it.

Trust him.

He walked over to the sofa, sat down. After a moment, he pulled his legs up on it, and put them on one side of Robbie.

He closed his eyes.

"What are you doing?" she sputtered.

"Making sure you don't go anywhere before we get things straightened out with the donkey."

"You can trust me," she said sweetly.

"Yeah, well, you can trust me to, but it appears you're not going to." He took his hat off the floor and put it full over his face. "Could you call your sisters and let them know you're okay?"

After a long time, he heard her move by him, go into her bedroom and close the curtain.

He wasn't aware he'd been holding his breath, until he started to breathe again.

She could have still left. She had stayed on the flimsiest of excuses.

Which meant, somewhere in that heart, she wanted to stay.

He lay awake for a long time, thinking, of how his life had led him to this moment. The bald-faced truth was that before his sister had gotten ill, he had been the most selfish of men.

So much so that he hadn't even been aware of his own selfishness.

But he had taken what he needed from life, and not put a whole lot back. He had not wasted any of his energy thinking of things beyond his own backyard. He had his horses and his business and that had been good enough. Oh, he'd been attracted to wild things, to frightened things, even back then. But it had never been about them.

It had been about him. About his great big ego liking to succeed where no one else could, where everyone else had failed.

Now that he thought about it, he supposed he and Barbara had been a better match at that point in his life than he had known.

Shallow. Selfish. Caught up, both of them, in the acquisition of their trinkets, the pursuit of dreams that had nothing to do with becoming better people or making a better world.

Nothing.

And then his sister had gotten sick.

And he had cried to the heavens: Why? Why her? Why this little boy? Why me?

And he knew he would never totally have those answers.

But tonight he felt a little bit of the why. His pain had made him bigger than he was before. A man able to understand pain in others, reach out his hand toward it, instead of backing away.

His sister leaving this world, and him becoming responsible for his nephew had helped him be able to do something he had never done before—give instead of take.

And now he would bring this gift that had given him—that had led him to this precise moment—and offer it to Corrine.

And let her make the choice.

Whether to take it or leave it.

He was going to hope that furious slamming going on in her bedroom was a good sign.

Chapter Ten

Matt woke up. He had a kink in his neck. Big surprise. Her couch wasn't made to be slept on. At least not by anyone over five feet high.

He glanced down at the other end of the couch. And frowned. The place where Robbie had slept was empty, the blanket in a heap on the floor.

"Robbie?"

He sat up, listened for sounds. Cupboard doors closing, water running in the bathroom. Nothing. Matt picked up the blanket. When he couldn't find the book Robbie had clung to last night, he felt his first twinge of nervousness.

He got up and did a quick inventory of the whole cottage. He even peeked behind the curtain to her bedroom.

She sat up on her elbow and looked at him. At any other time, he might have savored that sight—her eyes on him drowsy, her animosity from last night not quite awake yet.

"I'm looking for Robbie."

Then he noticed the front door was open just a crack. Not even possible. That was one of the first rules he'd

laid down when Robbie came to stay with him. He didn
go wandering around the ranch before anybody got up i
the morning. The rule had been made after Matt had gotte
up one morning to a feeling eerily similar to this one. C
emptiness.

He opened the door, and stood on her porch, ran a han
through his hair.

"Robbie?" he called, and then louder, "Robbie?"

Nothing seemed to be stirring.

Corrine came out behind him, wrapping a housecoa
around her. Not the same girl who had sat on those step
in her nightgown and sneakers.

"What's wrong?"

"I don't know where Robbie is."

"What? He must be with the donkey."

Both of them looked toward the barn, and then Ma
remembered he had let the donkey out yesterday. With h
mare. And he could see the mare from here. But no dor
key.

He swore under his breath.

"What?"

"I think he's taken the donkey and gone somewhere."

"But why?"

"I think he woke up last night while we were, er, talk
ing."

She went pale before his eyes. "He wouldn't care tha
I was leaving," she whispered.

"Oh, sure," he snapped. "He's gotten used to losin
everything he cares about by now." He felt like he'd h
her, the hurt was so intense in her face.

"You two are better off without me," she said.

"Why is that?"

"Because I'm not—" she drew a deep shudderin
breath. "Nobody can love me."

"Not if you don't let them," he agreed, scanning the
yard.

"Matt, I *know*," she said, her voice low. "I've been in
and out of foster homes since I was six. My own aunt
couldn't bear me."

"You don't *know* anything," he told her with quiet fury.

"I've been arrested, too."

He could see the shame in her eyes, and the terror.
There. Her worst secrets out. She had told him. Finally.

"For what?" he asked her.

"I was sixteen. I took some things that weren't mine."

"Oh, for God's sake," he said. "Is that what you do?
Make everything about you ten times, a hundred times
worse than it really is, so you can feel sorry for yourself?
I spent a night in jail once myself. I was seventeen and
drunk. It was a long time ago, and I've managed to forgive
myself."

"You don't understand."

"Yes, I do, Corrine."

"I can't be part of your future. And Robbie's. I don't
know how."

"Fine. How about if you tell him that when we find
him?" He pushed by her and went back in the house,
pulled on his boots. Not looking at her, he took a deep
breath. "It's not your fault he's gone."

"Just tell me what I need to do now."

"He may not be far. Let's just go have a look around."

They went together, calling, beating down the grass,
looking under logs. No Robbie and no donkey.

Which meant he must have gotten away earlier than
Matt thought. Because it would be pretty hard to hide the
donkey.

How had Robbie persuaded the donkey to leave his lady
love?

"Did your mare find her own way in there?" Corri■ asked, a worry on top of the worry.

"No. I put her there. I was tired of her sulking and hi braying."

"You put them together? But I thought—" her voi■ drifted away.

She thought his damn horses and his property mea■ everything to him. More than her. He reached out an touched her shoulder.

"Sometimes things just are meant to be. And it's n■ up to me to get in the way of them." And he wasn't talki■ about a donkey. Or just about himself, either.

She jerked away from his touch, but even so he notice■ as they searched, that the defensiveness was falling awa from her, her strength and beauty shining through.

She kept calm. Lots of experience dealing with crisi Would a day ever come when she would see the trut■ Her early heartbreaks had given her every gift she no■ had: her creativity, her great strength of spirit, the sens tivity that made her so defensive?

"Maybe I'm going about this wrong," he said. "Let go back to your place and I'll see if I can pick up a track.■

Sure enough in the worn dirt of her road, he found ther One small sneaker print, one large unshod untrimmed ho■ print.

"He took the road. Where the hell is he going? Hop the truck."

She did, without questioning. A small trust. If he ma■ too big a deal of it, she might bolt and run for good. ■ ignored her and put the truck in gear.

She sat beside him in the truck. He'd asked her to con■ with him. No, assumed she would come with him. Want■ her to come with him.

And he knew everything now.

Had she made everything more than it was? Was she eling sorry for herself? Was she going to throw away r chance at happiness over things that were done and ne?

He slowed the truck, slammed it into neutral, hopped t. She watched him trace a track with his fingers, hold dirt to his nose, squint into the distance.

He could track, just like a scout in an old Western vie. How many people, in this day and age, could track? But Matt Donahue wasn't really from this day and age all.

He was from a slower time, a harder time, a simpler ne, when men were strong and tough and honest.

"He's heading toward town." He got back in the truck, face set in a grim line.

She felt sick about Robbie. It was her fault. It had al- ys been her fault.

"Please don't make this about you."

She started and looked at him, but he was focused in- tly, driving slowly, watching both sides of the road, metimes stopping to look into the distance.

Don't make this about you.

He meant for her not to blame herself. But instead, she w a different truth. It was always about her. What she s thinking and feeling and believing.

And suddenly she knew what love was.

It was the ability to make it about other people.

It was about being able to give something to them, to se this terrible self-focus she had picked up like a virus en she'd returned to Minneapolis.

Maybe all of life was as simple as Abby had made it m, once upon a time, a long time ago.

Could it be that simple? Leaving the past behind, and

not looking to the future at all? As simple as believin
today good things could happen? To her?

But good things had not happened!

Robbie was missing.

But Abby had said, too, that sometimes the things th
seemed bad could turn out to be good in the end. If Robb
had not been gone this morning, would she have lost a
time in packing her bag, getting away from them?

From the terrible ache and yearning that being arou
them stirred to life in her?

It occurred to her, like a light going on in a dark tunn
that Robbie needed her. No one had ever needed her b
fore. Not really.

But he did.

She slid Matt a look. And he needed her, too.

Oh, he was big and hard and self-sufficient. And dyi
of loneliness. He needed softness and laughter. He need
to know life didn't take away every single good thing.

She thought of him losing his sister.

He could not lose his nephew, too.

Or her.

She slid across the seat, until her thigh touched his thig
and her shoulder touched his, and he turned his head a
looked at her, and a little smile chased the worry from h
eyes.

"Welcome home," he said softly.

"Matt," she started laughing, and crying, "there he is.

Sure enough, in the distance, Robbie was walking dow
the middle of the road, his steps dragging, the donkey fo
lowing placidly behind him. He heard the truck and mov
over to the left hand shoulder, without turning around.

Matt pulled up beside him, and unrolled his window.

Corrine saw that Robbie was dragging her great big su

se. She was glad she had not had time to throw more in

Robbie looked straight ahead.

"You need a ride, buddy?" Matt asked.

Robbie's cheeks were stained with tears. He shook his
ad, stubbornly.

"Leaving home?" Matt asked.

Robbie nodded.

"Can I come?" Matt asked softly. "No point me going
me without you. It wouldn't be home anymore."

Robbie had to ponder this development. He sent his un-
 a sidelong look, scowled when he saw Corrine in the
ck.

"Can I come, too?" Corrine asked. "I see you already
cked my suitcase."

"I knew you wouldn't go without it. And our donkey."

"So," she shrugged, "everything I care about is right
re on this road. I guess I better come along." An odd
incidence, that on a lonely stretch of road twenty-four
ars ago, she had lost everything. Her mother. Her father.
r sisters.

And now, on a lonely stretch of road, thousands of miles
ay, she was being given everything.

"Matt, pull over," she said.

He pulled over and parked the truck. He got out, and
ld out his hand to her. He looked in her eyes for a long
oment, and then he kissed her, lightly on the lips.

They ran to catch up to Robbie. She took one of his
nds. Matt took the lead rope away from Robbie with one
nd and took his hand with his other.

They walked along in silence for awhile, up a long hill.
Robbie peeked up at his uncle, and then at her. "So,"
 said, finally, "where are we going?"

"You're in charge of this," Matt said. "You decide."

"Is Corrie still going to go away?"

"No. I've decided to stick around."

"I have a peanut butter sandwich. We could stop, a
I'll share it with you."

"Are you hungry, Corrie?" Matt asked her deadpan.

"Starving," she replied, as they crested the hill. Belo
them she could see Miracle Harbor, the town's hous
looking like matchboxes scattered around the cove. A
beyond the town, the ocean, deep and blue and quiet a
going on forever.

They walked off into the long grass beside the ditc
Matt tied the donkey to a fence post and sat down.

Robbie opened the suitcase.

A peanut butter sandwich was squished in on top of t
few items she had thrown in there last night.

Last night, she had stopped believing in miracles. B
wasn't this a miracle?

It was the only one that counted really. The miracle
sitting in peace in the tall grass, with the people you love
most in the world around you. Could a girl like her, wh
had never known such moments, ask for anything else?

She watched Robbie carefully dividing the sandwich
four.

"Four?" Matt said.

"The donkey," Robbie told his uncle.

"I think it's time to name that donkey," she said. "I'
going to call him Mister Miracle."

"Oh," Robbie breathed, "that's perfect."

She looked at her donkey, who was watching them o
of the corner of his eye. Yes, it was perfect. All the aspec
of her life coming together because she was learning
care. To commit.

Naming the donkey was like saying, *I'm staying. You'
stuck with me.*

And Matt heard the words not spoken. He took his sand-
ch and held it up.

"A toast," he said.

"What's a toast?" Robbie asked.

So they explained to him what a toast usually was. But
y toasted with peanut butter instead, bumping their
dwiches together.

"A toast," Matt said, and his eyes became very serious.
o miracles."

They ate the sandwiches. Robbie ate the donkey's por-
n after Mister Miracle made it plain he preferred grass.

"I heard you talking last night," Robbie said, pulling
t a blade of grass and sticking it between his two
mbs, blowing ineffectually. "I pretended I was sleep-
, but I wasn't. I heard Corrie say she was going away.
aited until you went to sleep, Aunt—I mean, Uncle—
d then I went and got Mister Miracle."

Matt pulled out a blade of grass, stuck it between his
o thumbs and blew. A piercing whistle resulted. "So, I
to be uncle, now, huh?"

"I have an auntie now."

"Do you?" Matt asked.

"Corrie's going to be my auntie."

"Hey, pint-size, you're showing my hand," Matt said
ffly.

"Brandy ran away in the book. And it worked. So I
ided to try it, too."

Corrine shifted, sat cross-legged, pulled Robbie into her
. "Brandy isn't real, honey."

"Yes, she is," Robbie and Matt said together.

"What?"

"She's you," Robbie said.

"She's you," Matt said. "Can't you see that?"

And all of a sudden she could. She could see that, just

like the character she had created, her life had given her
great gifts. Resourcefulness. Wit. Compassion. Strength

Brandy loved everybody.

And suddenly, so did, Corrine.

"Are you crying, Auntie?" Robbie asked.

She nodded, unable to speak, felt Matt's arms go arou
her, circle her.

And just like that, they were a family, sitting in the lo
grass.

"Are you sad?" Robbie asked, touching her tears.

"No," she said, looking at Matt. "I'm happy."

Robbie got up. "Grown-ups are pretty weird. Mist
Miracle wants to go home now. He likes Cupie Doll."

"I'll walk home with you and Mister Miracle," Corri
said. "Matt can take the truck."

"Nah, I'm walking home, too. I'll come back for t
truck later." He got up, and swung Robbie onto his shou
ders. She untied the donkey, and Matt slipped his ha
around her waist.

Only a few days ago she had thought that there w
nothing as magical as being part of a couple.

But now she felt a deeper magic, a truer magic.

And that was being part of this.

A family of three.

The donkey nudged her with his nose, indignant.

"Okay," she said, "four."

After she contacted her sisters to let them know she w
okay, they spent the day together, laughing and playi
games, sitting on her front porch. In quiet moments, sh
told Matt about her life. About the puppy she hadn't be
allowed to keep, and the jacket she'd had to share, and t
lines she'd had to write.

And with each thing she told him, she felt more fre
And watched the most astounding thing happen.

His love for her didn't diminish.

She could feel it growing as she trusted him with all
that she had been and was.

"I've got chores to do at home," he said, finally, reluc-
antly.

She hated to let him go. Hated it.

"Come for dinner tonight. At my place," he said.

She smiled. It was like a final test. Everything, so far
had been on her territory, in her control. "Okay."

She'd never been to his house before. It was the next
driveway up from hers, but at the top of the hill instead
of at the base of it, as hers was.

She passed under the sign that said No Quarter Asked.
She stopped and looked at it. Sometime very recently,
a big white *S* had been taped over the *K* in asked.

She laughed out loud.

His place was beautiful. White fences, and a long white
barn, horses running over lush green pastures, colts and
fillies at their mothers sides.

When she got out of her jeep she looked behind her.
and could see all of Miracle Harbor in the distance.

His house was a big, old farmhouse. It was painted
white and had green shutters and a porch that wrapped
around three sides of it. It had seen generations of Donahues come and go. Babies had been born in this house,
and children had swung in the tire swing under the spreading branches of that huge oak.

It was the kind of house that a girl who had never experienced anything lasting needed to see.

The sidewalk had flowers growing in the border leading
up to the door. The storm door was open. She knocked on
the screen.

"Come in," he called.

She entered, feeling nervous. It was just her and M.
and Robbie. What was there to feel nervous about?

She stood in the entrance, looking into the living roor
He came and stood in the doorway to the kitchen, tea tow
thrown over his shoulder.

"I like the flowers outside," she said. "Somehow
can't see you planting flowers, Matt."

"I didn't. My sister did. She said they stood for hop
Come in."

Hope, that most precious and fearsome of human con
modities. She went in. His house felt just like a hou
should.

There were toys on the floor and books on the shelv
and magazines open on the coffee table. The furnitu
looked like furniture people actually liked and used. A l

His house was not the kind of house where you werer
allowed to touch, and everything in it was about how
looked.

No, his house was a home.

And everything in it was about how it felt.

She followed him into the kitchen. He was tossing sala
and had steaks ready to grill. Two steaks.

She cast a glance at the little kitchen table. It had ca
dles on it and was set for two.

"Where's Robbie?" she asked.

"Uh, your sister took him for the night."

"Good God. Not Brit, I hope."

"As a matter of fact, yeah. She's got them both. Yo
niece Belle, and Robbie."

"Thank God Mitch is there."

"That's what she said, too."

They both laughed quietly at the thought of Brit wi
kids.

"Brit said to tell you Angela looked quite a bit bett

hen they left her yesterday. Jordan had a bed moved into
e room so he could be with her. Does that mean some-
ing to you?''

She smiled. She had called Angela before she had come
re, and had heard the lightness in her voice.

She had thanked her for the gift she had carried safely
r twenty-four years. She thanked her for keeping the
omise she had made to her mother.

In the background, just before she had hung up, she had
ard Jordan's voice, and caught Angela's laughter.

To her that laughter meant the miracle of love never
opped. It didn't have any age limits, or any limits at all.
anything could heal Angela, make her completely better,
would be Jordan's love.

''Here,'' Matt said. He handed her a big parcel.

''What's this?''

''It's for you.''

''Me?'' She was not accustomed to being on the re-
iving end of gifts. She looked at it suspiciously, looked
vay.

''Aren't you going to open it?''

She took it on her lap, undid the paper. She noticed,
ith a smile, that it had been wrapped clumsily.

Inside were sheets.

The most beautiful sheets she had ever seen. Pure white
nen, with an eyelet border.

She gulped, wondering if this meant what she thought
did.

''Are we picking up that kiss, tonight, where it left off?''
e whispered, suddenly looking at his lips, being achingly
vare of how alone they were, how free.

''No, ma'am, we sure aren't.''

She stared at him, baffled, hurt.

''The sheets are your first wedding present. From me.''

"Wedding?"

"Yes, ma'am, and I'm keeping my hands off of yo
until we've done it right."

She put her nose in the sheets and bit back the tear
Wouldn't she know it? Her old-fashioned man was goin
to be old-fashioned right until the end.

"You can cry if you want to, " he said. He came u
behind her, and put his hand on her neck, rubbed his thum
along the tense muscles. "And here I vowed I was goin
to keep my hands off you. Will you marry me, Corrie
Please?"

It was that *please* that got her. A man who could hav
anything in the whole world, and he acted like having he
would be the best. The most unbelievable wonderful be
thing in the whole world.

Corrine Parsons.

She turned, stood up, and found herself in his arms. Sh
kissed him all over. She kissed his face and his throat an
opened the buttons on his shirt and kissed his chest.

"Yes," she said. "Yes, yes, yes."

"Could you just give me a clear answer?" he teased.

And then he kissed her back, kissed her until the lin
of earth blurred and she could not tell what was earth any
more and what was heaven.

"When?" she sighed against him.

"As soon as is humanly possible. Your sister Abby sai
she'd take advantage of Belle being gone and sew a
night."

"You told my sisters?"

"Your sisters know everything. Brit just took one loo
at me when I dropped off Robbie and was jumping up an
down screaming. She had the other one on the phone i
the blink of an eye."

Her sisters knew everything.

Her sisters, who had known who she was before she knew herself. Her sisters who had loved her until she could love herself.

Just like this man.

Who would help her mine the coal of her past until it glittered with diamonds.

"Kiss me again," she pleaded.

"No, ma'am," he said, backing playfully away from her.

Laughing, with a laughter that seemed to come right from her soul, she chased him, until they were both breathless, and he collapsed on his living room floor, and she collapsed on top of him.

And when his arms went around her, she did glimpse the future in the dark wonder of his eyes as he looked at her. She felt it, when he pushed back a wisp of her hair with his thumb.

She had three rules she had lived by: never cry, never hope for better, never let anyone see she was scared.

She felt the tears, whispered to him that she was just a little bit scared, and saw all the tenderness she had ever hoped for in his eyes.

Firmly, she bid her rules goodbye.

And said hello to a brand-new world.

Epilogue

"I'm crying all ready," Brit sniffled, looking back over her shoulder down the church aisle, "and they haven' even started playing the music. She looks absolutely beau tiful in that white confection. Doesn't she?"

"She does," her sister agreed dreamily.

"I just love that silk trouser idea. Mitch, we might have to renew our vows, so that I can wear something like that."

"We've only been married two months and three days," Mitch said drily, but he gave his wife an indulgent look.

"Look," Abby whispered, the tears rolling down he cheeks, now, too.

The music had finally started. Robbie, dressed in a little black suit, and with Belle's hand firmly in his grasp, began to walk up the aisle. He was very patient with the little tyke who toddled along beside him in her white ruffle dress.

Corrine bit back her own tears, felt the hand tighten or hers, and turned to the man who sat beside her in the pew

Belle suddenly tripped and fell, and sat in the aisle cry

g. The music stopped, while they got her organized gain.

Corrine leaned over and said to her sisters, "Did I tell ou we're expecting?"

"What?" Her sisters, whose attention had been riveted n the back door of the church, now turned and stared at er.

"A little mule," she said happily. "Next spring. Cupie oll and Mister Miracle."

"Matt Donahue," Brit hissed, "would you control your ife? This is no place for a discussion on animal hus- andry."

"I'll do my best," Matt said insincerely.

Corrine grinned at him. This was one of the things she as discovering about herself. She was mischievous—a uality that had been mistaken for bad most of her life. e winked at her. She knew it was one of the things he ked best about her.

The music started again, and the children made it to the ont with no further incident.

Angela Pondergrove stepped out of the alcove at the ack of the church, her eyes on the man who stood, tall nd distinguished and silver-haired, waiting for her at the tar.

She floated up the aisle.

The white silk pantsuit looked glorious on her. Corrine ad been so honored when Angela had asked her if she ould mind if the slack suit was her "something bor- wed."

And of course, she hadn't at all. She loved the idea of at wedding outfit being used again, bringing someone se that joy and confidence of being an absolute princess r the day.

It was at Corrine and Matt's own quiet wedding that

Angela had made her announcement that she and Jordan planned to get married.

"Just a short while ago," she had told them, "I thought I was dying. I felt so weighted down. But each day after I told you about the promise I made to your mother, I felt better and stronger. When Corrine called and thanked me for keeping your mother's gift safe for the three of you for twenty-four years, I felt alive again.

"I feel like I was guided by the love of Belle Parsons. And that I did the best I knew how to do. And that the legacy of love is the truest of all legacies, the one that will not and cannot be put asunder.

"I am so fortunate. To have had a man like Alf love me.

"And now Jordan. The ability to accept this second love is the gift the three of you gave to me."

Matt reached over, and brushed the tears from Corrine's eyes. She caught his fingers and kissed her own teardrops off of them. Her eyes met his.

"You know," he whispered, "for the longest time I wasn't certain what I believed about anything, anymore."

"And now?"

He didn't answer. He just smiled. And his smile was the smile of a man who believed. Totally. With all his heart.

In the infinite and saving power of love.

*   *   *   *   *

Modern Romance™
...seduction and
passion guaranteed

Tender Romance™
...love affairs that
last a lifetime

Medical Romance™
...medical drama
on the pulse

Historical Romance™
...rich, vivid and
passionate

Sensual Romance™
...sassy, sexy and
seductive

Blaze Romance™
...the temperature's
rising

27 new titles every month.

Live the emotion

MILLS & BOON®

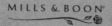

MILLS & BOON

dark angel
LYNNE GRAHAM

Knight in shining armour
or avenging angel?

Available from 21st March 2003

Available at most branches of WH Smith,
Tesco, Martins, Borders, Eason, Sainsbury's
and all good paperback bookshops.

0403/135/MB68

FREE
2 BOOKS
AND A SURPRISE GIFT!

We would like to take this opportunity to thank you for reading this Mills & Boon® book offering you the chance to take TWO more specially selected titles from the Modern Romance series absolutely FREE! We're also making this offer to introduce you to the benefits the Reader Service™ —

★ FREE home delivery   ★ FREE gifts and competitions
★ FREE monthly Newsletter   ★ Exclusive Reader Service discount
★ Books available before they're in the shops

Accepting these FREE books and gift places you under no obligation to buy; you may cancel at any time, even after receiving your free shipment. Simply complete your details below and return the entire page to the address below. **You don't even need a stamp!**

YES! Please send me 2 free Modern Romance™ books and a surprise gift. I understand that unless you hear from me, I will receive 4 superb new titles every month for just £2.00 each, postage and packing free. I am under no obligation to purchase any books and may cancel my subscription at any time. The free books and gift will be mine to keep in any case.

P3ZE

Ms/Mrs/Miss/Mr ....Initials ....
BLOCK CAPITALS PLEASE

Surname ....

Address ....

....

....Postcode ....

Send this whole page to:
UK: FREEPOST CN81, Croydon, CR9 3WZ
EIRE: PO Box 4546, Kilcock, County Kildare (stamp required)